14 DAYS TO LOVE

14 SHORT SWEET STEAMY NOVELLAS

LAURA (L.A.) MARIANI

THE PEOPLE ALCHEMIST

ISBN: 978-1-917104-11-1

BOOKS BY LAURA (L.A.)MARIANI

Holiday Romance

14 Days to Love Series: Short Sweet Steamy

Parisian Serendipity

Venetian Whispers

Mumbay Surprise

Romeo in Rome

New York Melody

Artic Embrace

Santorini Sunsets

Havana Heat

Barcelona Dreams

Marrakesh Magic

Vienna Waltz

Sydney Sparks

Amsterdam Affair

Cape Town Safari

Twelve Days of Christmas Series

A Partridge in a Pear Tree: Hot Spicy Christmas Novella

Two Turtle Doves: Hot Spicy Christmas Novella

Three French Hens: Hot Spicy Christmas Novella

Four Calling Birds: Hot Spicy Christmas Novella

Five Golden Rings: Hot Spicy Christmas Novella

Six Geese a-Laying: Hot Spicy Christmas Novella

Seven Swans a-Swimming: Hot Spicy Christmas Novella

Eight Maids a-Milking: Hot Spicy Christmas Novella

Nine Ladies Dancing: Hot Spicy Christmas Novella

Ten Lords a-Leaping: Hot Spicy Christmas Novella

Eleven Pipers Piping: Hot Spicy Christmas Novella

Twelve Drummers Drumming: Hot Spicy Christmas Novella

Box Set

Twelve Days of Christmas

Shadowbrook Paranormal Series

A Halloween Romance: Enchanted in Shadowbrook

The Midnight Hour:A Halloween Shadowbrook Romance

Navy Seals Hunks Series

SEALed Hearts

SEALed with a Kiss

SEALed Undercover

SEALed Pursuit

SEALed Love Code

SEALed beyond Duty

A Royal Romance Trilogy

A Coronation Weekend Romance

The Wicked Princess

The Lost Kingdom

The Nine Lives of Gabrielle Series

Gabrielle (prequel/first in series)

For Three She Plays

A New York Adventure

Searching for Goren

Tasting Freedom

For Three She Strays

Paris Toujours Paris

Me Myself and Us

Freedom Over Me

For Three She Stays

London Calling

Back in Your Arms

The Greatest Love

Box Sets

For Three She Plays - Book 1-3

For Three She Strays - Book 4-6

For Three She Stays - Book 7-9

The Nine Lives of Gabrielle Book 1-9 + 3 Bonus stories

FOREWORD

14 Days To Love is a collection of steamy romance novellas that are intended for a mature audience.

Dive into a world where passion knows no boundaries and love blossoms in the most enchanting corners of the globe with 14 standalone short stories that promise to ignite your imagination and set your heart aflutter. A captivating blend of steamy encounters, wanderlust-infused adventures, and irresistibly sweet endings.

Wanderlust Around the World: From the snowy peaks of the Alps to the sultry streets of Havana, "14 Days to Love" whisks you away to exotic locales where love blooms amidst the cultural tapestry of each destination. Immerse yourself in the magic of diverse landscapes, from the Arctic's icy beauty to the vibrant heart of Mumbai.

Steamy Short Romance: For romance enthusiasts who crave quick escapes into the realm of passion, these short stories deliver an irresistible blend of sizzling chemistry, alpha males, and fierce heroines. Lose yourself in tales of love at first sight, where sparks fly, and emotions run high.

PARISIAN SERENDIPITY

PROLOGUE
ELIZABETH

I jam the last tubes of oil paint into my worn duffel bag with a frustrated grunt. The colorful tubes knock against each other, creating a chaotic melody that matches the turmoil in my mind. My hands, usually steady and sure when holding a paintbrush, tremble with anger and hurt.

"Paris," I can taste the promise on my lips as I whisper it to myself. It is a city that doesn't just accept art but embraces art like a lover. Unlike him, who looks at my canvases and sees only wasted wall space.

His scoffing laugh echoes in my head, followed by his dismissive words that cut deep into my soul. "It's a nice hobby, Liz," he said with a careless shrug, and I felt the sting of betrayal in his words. He never really believed in me.

. . .

"Damn you," I mutter, and I'm not sure if I'm talking to him or to the fear gnawing at my resolve. Enough. I zip the bag shut, a satisfying rasp that seals away the past.

My fingers twitch, craving the rough texture of charcoal and the satisfying drag as it brings my ideas to life on paper. The urge to paint Paris consumes me; I need to capture its vibrant lights and elusive shadows, to feel them dance under my skin and bleed onto the canvas until love- or some pale imitation of it-pours out.

I pace through the empty apartment, the cold hardwood floors chilling my bare feet. The air is tinged with the sharp scent of turpentine and broken promises. The walls are stripped bare, except for one painting that stands out like a sore thumb - a bold mix of reds and golds that never fit into his minimalist aesthetic. He prefers muted tones, polite conversations, and a girlfriend who is content being less than she dreams of.

"Goodbye," I say to the empty room, to his ghost that lingers in the corners. It feels right, like the first stroke on a blank canvas. There's no response, of course. There never was, not really.

I sling the strap of my bag over my shoulder, feeling the weight of my entire world in that canvas holdall. Keys clink as I drop them on the counter, their metallic chime singing of finality.

· · ·

His voice rings in my ears, tinged with arrogance and superiority."If you are going, there is no coming back," he sneered. "You'll never make it; you're just a small-town waitress from Pittsburgh for crying out loud!"

"Watch me," I shoot back, locking the door behind me. The click is a gunshot. Freedom. The hallway blurs as I make for the stairs, adrenaline pumping through my veins.

"Art will feed you, Liz," I tell myself because belief is a meal I've been starving for. My heart aches for it, hungry for strokes of brilliance on my terms.

As I descend the narrow stairwell of the apartment building, I can feel the excitement building in my chest. Ahead lies the unknown, a city famed for lovers and dreamers. The thought of it fans the embers in my chest into a blaze. No more dimming my fire for someone who can't stand the heat.

"Paris," The word fills me with determination and purpose. And it's not just a name—a battle cry to claim my destiny with every step. And for the first time in years, I feel truly alive. Homeless and jobless, yes, but most importantly, free.

1

ELIZABETH

Charles de Gaulle is a cacophony of sounds to my ears. Everyone is hurrying around and speaking so fast that my head is spinning.

"Gare Du Nord s'il vous plaît?" I ask in my pigeon French.

"Bon, Il y a des taxis, le RoissyBus, les lignes de bus 350+351 et le RER B".

"Sorry…Mmmh… En anglais? Do you speak English?" from the look on his face, I feel ashamed I have even asked.

"Sure," and he repeats himself. It is now daunting on me that doing an Emily in Paris might be more challenging than it sounded.

· · ·

I buy a ticket for the RER B train and find a seat by the window. The train lurches forward, and I watch the scenery pass by as we make our way to Paris. As the train pulls into the bustling Gare Du Nord, I grip my bag tightly and step off onto the platform. The sounds of French chatter and train announcements fill my ears as I make my way to my bed and breakfast. I am exhausted from the journey and quickly collapse onto the soft bed.

The metallic tang of Parisian air licks my lips as I step out of the hotel on the cobblestones. I decide to just stroll and get lost. The uneven cobblestone streets guide my steps as I meander through the City. A Roman Catholic church, Église Saint-Vincent-de-Paul, catches my eye with its beautiful architecture and ivy-covered walls. Intrigued, I stop to sketch it for a while.

As I continue my walk, I come across Rue Montorgueil, a bustling street filled with local shops, cafes, and bakeries. The aroma of freshly baked croissants wafts through the air, tempting me to stop and indulge. I take my time wandering, soaking up the atmosphere and watching locals going about their day. This feels like the real Paris, away from tourist traps and crowded landmarks.

I stroll down the street, past blooming gardens and quaint cafes, until I reach Rue Du Pont Neuf. The sound of rushing water leads me to the majestic River Seine, and as I walk along its banks, I come across the famous Love Locks adorning the bridges. Across another bridge and a few more blocks, I enter Rue Saint Dominique. This street seems frozen in time with its medieval architecture and bustling activity. Halfway up, I pause to admire the manicured gardens of Cathedral Saint Louis des Invalides. And then, like magic, I see the top of the Eiffel Tower poking out from the buildings, closer and closer, until I stumble upon the lady herself! The Eiffel Tower pierces the sky, an iron sentinel watching over this City of Love.

My heart quickens with excitement and nervousness as I embark on this solo journey of self-discovery. Tourists are taking pictures everywhere. I sit down and start sketching again.

"Excusez-moi, mademoiselle," a deep voice interrupts my daydreaming, and I turn to find deep, dark eyes locked onto mine. He stands before me, a hint of a five o'clock shadow framing his chiseled jaw. French men are definitely not my type—too smooth, too polished, too arrogant, and I don't need more arrogant men in my life—but there's an undeniable pull, magnetic and unnerving.

"American?" he inquires, one eyebrow arching in a challenge that stirs something defiant within me.

I shrug, I thought I had done my best to look as Parisian and understated as possible, "Guilty," I retort, tilting my chin up, meeting his gaze dead-on.

"Most Americans come here searching for something—love, perhaps?" His tone is playful, yet there's a guarded edge as if he's used to women who want more than just conversation.His English is impeccable with a seductive French accent, far too sexy for my own good.

"Maybe we're just looking for a good croissant," I shoot back, my walls fortified against men who think money buys everything, even affection.

We're locked in a dance of words, our banter flaring like the sparks from clashing swords. I can feel the electricity between us pulsing. It's as if the space between us is tangible, crackling with the promise of something more.

Stop it, Liz; he is a Frenchman; they all flirt all the time.

"Ah, but one can find both if they're lucky." He steps closer, and my pulse quickens, betraying my outward coolness.

"Or skilled," I counter, unwilling to concede.

"Bien sûr." He smiles, a slow, dangerous curve of his lips. Our eyes lock, and Paris blurs into the background.

"Enjoy your search, mademoiselle," he says, stepping away, leaving a void where his presence once burned.

• • •

"Same to you, monsieur," I call after him, my voice steady though my heart isn't.

With a last glance at the symbol of romance towering over us, I reach into my purse—and freeze. The pocket where I'd stashed my money, credit cards, and passport gaped open, empty. Panic claws up my throat, sharp and suffocating.

"Sugar," I curse under my breath, frantically searching every compartment with shaking hands. Gone. All gone.

2

———

GUILLAUME

I weave through the crowded streets of Paris, my face hidden behind a dark scarf and sunglasses. I love getting lost in the city, but it's becoming more difficult with the influx of tourists. As I approach Tour Montparnasse, I decide to make a quick detour to Rue Cler for a croissant from Ronde des Pains.

I spot her as I turn down the charming street lined with cafes and shops. Her red beret and glossy brown hair stand out among the crowd. She's clearly trying to blend in as a Parisian, but something about her screams American and catches my attention, and before I know it, I'm striking up a conversation with her. She's quick-witted and keeps me on my toes. But beneath her confident facade, there's a slight hint of vulnerability. Suddenly, all I want to do is wrap her in my arms and protect her from the world.

My stomach churns with the thought of leaving her alone in this crowded tourist spot. I politely say goodbye and turn away, but I can't resist the urge to glance back at her one last time. As I do, I notice a shady figure eyeing her handbag.

My heart races as I sprint towards her, dodging through the throngs of tourists.

"Are you okay?" I ask breathlessly as I reach her side.

Tears are streaming down her face as she sobs, "Gone. All gone: my passport, my credit card, and cash." My heart aches for her as I see the devastation written all over her face.

"My phone," she cries, "he got my phone too! What am I going to do?"

Anger boils within me as I curse the thief under my breath. All I want to do is wrap her up in my arms and protect her from anyone who dares to harm her. But for now, I can only try to find a solution to this unfortunate situation. The bastard won't get away with this.

"Mademoiselle, let me take you to the police station to report the theft; there's one nearby," she nods. "I am Guil-laume, by the way," I say as I hold my hand out.

"Elizabeth," she says. Her skin is soft and clammy.

. . .

"Une seconde, s'il vous plait," I say before I move away to make a call and ask my secretary to cancel meetings for the rest of the day.

Elizabeth's eyes dart around nervously. "Do you have the number for your bank?" I ask gently. "You need to cancel the credit cards as soon as possible."

She fumbles in her purse and pulls out a small red notebook. "Please don't cry," I say, trying to comfort her. "We'll get everything sorted out."

"Do you want me to call someone for you? Your boyfriend?" I keep my fingers crossed.

"I haven't got one." She opens up to me about coming to Paris on a whim with her savings, her ex-boyfriend, and her dreams. Panic spreading within her.

"Let me help you." My heart aches for her as we spend the next few hours at the police station and making phone calls.

Finally, I ask her, "Let me cook you dinner. To cheer you up," she looks at me with those big brown eyes. "You need to eat."

. . .

Elizabeth hesitates.

"The police have my contact details," I add, hoping to reassure her.

"OK", she whispers timidly. My pulse quickens as we head towards my home away from home.

3

ELIZABETH

The narrow streets of Paris twist and turn, a labyrinth guiding us to Guillaime's sanctuary. My heart is a drumbeat in my ears, syncopated with the click of his shoes against cobblestones. The scent of the Seine mingles with the dusk, a hint of mystery on the breeze as he leads me deeper into his world.

He pushes open an unassuming door, and we step into the dimly lit warmth of a private haven. It's a room that speaks. He lits candles across the small place, and the amber glow flickers across his sharp features, dancing shadows on his jawline.

"Welcome to where I hide from the world," he murmurs, his voice a low rumble reverberating through my bones.

My pulse quickens as he pulls out a chair, a silent invitation. I sit, enveloped by the softness of velvet, my skin tingling with anticipation. The air between us crackles as he pours wine, its ruby color reflecting dark pools of longing in his eyes.

I can't resist exploring his apartment as Guillaume bustles in the small kitchen. The outside light spills through tall windows, casting specked light on the mismatched furniture and colorful decor. A menagerie of papier mâché masks smiles at me from above the doorway while a modern nude watercolor hangs near an old oil painting of cows grazing in a verdant field. An enormous gilt mirror leans against one wall, its glass speckled with age and too large to hang. Books are scattered everywhere, from Shakespeare and Hemingway to obscure French authors I have never heard of.

Feeling a sudden urge to use the bathroom, I find my way. But when I search for the familiar lever or button to flush, there is no such thing in sight. Baffled, I call out for instructions. Guillaume's inaudible shouts from the kitchen only confuse me more, so he comes in to show me how to work the alien gizmo. Mortified by this unexpected intimacy, I quickly close the lid when he enters.

When I return to the living area, I am astonished that he has set a perfectly staged table for two as if prepared for a special occasion. Formality and pomp always made me nervous, Michael was always so pompous. I beg him not to go through any trouble. His surprised expression makes me realize this is how things are done in France. Every detail carefully arranged to be aesthetically pleasing. Of course.

• • •

Our meal unfolds, each course a discovery, flavors bursting like fireworks, rich and decadent. With every bite, every sip, the space between us shrinks until the air is thick, with the heat of his eyes locked onto mine. Dessert is something sinfully chocolate, but it's nothing compared to the hunger in his stare. He reaches across, fingers brushing mine as he offers a taste, the contact igniting a fire within. I part my lips, and the sweet rush of dessert is second to his touch that lingers, deliberate, claiming.

"Elizabeth," he breathes, a whisper laden with desire.

The world narrows down to the stretch of silence as he leans in, his intent clear. Our first kiss is a spark that catches flame, passionate yet restrained. His lips command, coaxing a response from deep within me. He's a gentleman, holding back the full force of his want, giving me the power to break away.

But I don't.

I melt into him, the press of his mouth firm and insistent, our breaths mingling, a shared sigh. His hand finds the small of my back, a gentle pressure that pulls me closer, not letting me forget who guides this dance. Though the kiss deepens and his body speaks of a primal need, he keeps a careful distance. His respect for my safety and comfort is as palpable as the heat rolling off his skin.

· · ·

"Are you okay, ma chérie?" he asks when we part, his forehead resting against mine.

"More than okay," I whisper back, my voice steady despite the storm he stirs within me.

Wrapped in the magic of Parisian twilight, Guillaume is both a tempest and a refuge. And I am caught, willingly, in the eye of the storm.

4

GUILLAUME

The week passes by in a whirlwind. The US Embassy is arranging for a new passport. I speak to my good friend, the Commissaire, to help me with my deception and pretend they found the money when they arrested the thief.

I still can't believe she was carrying three thousand euros on her. Elizabeth was delighted and super impressed by the efficiency of the French police. Unfortunately, he was not so keen on letting me have some time with that bastard. But it doesn't matter now because she is safe and sound by my side. All I want to do is spoil her rotten and shower her with love and affection.

Our first kiss woke up a fire inside of me that I cannot extinguish and is growing with each moment I spend with her. I never want this to end. My defenses are crumbling down. Yet, I had to keep my emotions in check. She is still vulnerable from her breakup and ordeal.

· · ·

For now, I love showing her my Paris and watching her work on her canvas at night. She is so talented and deserves to be recognized. That's when the idea strikes me - perhaps some of my influential acquaintances can 'accidentally' discover her work. It is a long shot, but worth trying if it means getting her name out there.

The luminescent glow of my computer screen is a stark reminder that the night has plundered past midnight. My fingers fly over the keys, crafting emails like spells to ward off the looming crisis at work. The office is silent except for the occasional groan of the historic building settling deeper into its foundations—a symphony of dedication or perhaps obsession.

The lie sits heavy in my chest—a necessary evil. I pause and swivel in my chair to peer out at the Parisian skyline, a chiaroscuro of light and shadow that mirrors the duality of my life.

I let my thoughts drift to her—Elizabeth, my fierce American artist with eyes like dawn and a spirit untamed. I crave her presence. I am counting the days til the sweet surrender of her body against mine.

I stand, bones weary, muscles protesting, and stride to the window. Paris sleeps below, unaware of the tempest she stirs within me. A text vibrates my phone: a photo from her: a sketch, quick but intimate, of two figures entwined beneath the Eiffel Tower. It's us, a dream penned in graphite. Thank God she accepted my old phone. Not without protesting.

My thumb hovers, achingly close to confessing everything —the billions tucked away in accounts, the philanthropy, the media that trails my every move like a shadow. But no, not yet. This anonymity is a gift, a reprieve from the weight of expectations.

"Incroyable," I send back, the word an inadequate vessel for the torrent of my emotions.

"Goodnight, Guillaume," she responds, and I can almost feel her lips brushing against my cheek, a phantom caress that promises more.

I lock my phone, the sketch seared into my mind's eye. Tomorrow, I tell myself. But the web of lies tightens around me, each thread a shackle forged from fear and desire. Fear of losing her to the truth, desire to possess her completely, without the trappings of my status.

"Demain, Elizabeth," I whisper into the silence, a vow etched with longing. "Tomorrow."

5

ELIZABETH

The Parisian night is a seductress, all shadows and whispers, the Eiffel Tower twinkling in the distance. I am curled up alone on this plush chaise lounge that's too big for one, waiting for Guillaume to come back. Days are passing by like a flash. I log into my email on his laptop when I see a notification blink with his name—Michael.

I click it open, my heart hammering against my ribs. His words flicker on the screen, a litany of could-haves and should-haves. He speaks of regret, of lost time, but they're just echoes now, bouncing off the high ceilings of the empty apartment.

My fingers fly across the keyboard, crafting a reply. Each keystroke is a heartbeat, each sentence a step closer to the closure I crave. I'm not the woman I used to be, a mere silhouette fading into the background of his towering ambitions and disdain for mine.

• • •

"Michael," I begin, my voice a tremor in the quiet room, though I know he can't hear me. I pause, the cursor blinking impatiently. In the silence, the city seems to hold its breath.

But before I hit send another email. "Elizabeth, I'm in Paris. Can we meet?"

"Ten a.m., Hôtel de Soubise," I reply, closing the laptop with a soft click. I rise from the chaise, my movements sure and light. Closure.

6

GUILLAUME

As Elizabeth's heels click against the cobblestones, each step feels like a hammer striking my heart. The scent of blossoming jasmine fills the air, but it is her perfume that envelopes me - a seductive blend of vanilla and rebellion. I follow behind, my steps quieter.

She spins around, her expression a mix of surprise and fear, not unlike one of her vibrant paintings. "Guillaume? What are you doing here?"

I close the distance between us in long strides, our bodies almost touching. "I saw you with him, Elizabeth. With *him*." The words taste bitter on my tongue, burning with jealousy and betrayal.

"Who?" Her brows furrow, confusion lacing her tone, and something taut begins to fray somewhere inside.

• • •

"Your ex. The one who didn't see the fire in your brush strokes."

A harsh, humorless laugh bursts from her lips, cutting through the tension like a knife. "It's not what you think."

"Am I supposed to believe that?" My hands twitch at my sides, itching to reach out, to claim, to make sure she's truly here with me and not slipping back to some unworthy past.

"Oui," she says firmly. "Because it's true."

Her presence is a storm I never saw coming, disarming and fierce. I want to pull her close, press her against the nearest wall, and kiss her until all misunderstandings evaporate like mist over the Seine.

"Help me understand, then," I say, each word a stone laid down for her to cross back to me.

"Understand what?" She tilts her head, a challenge in her eyes.

"Understand why you'd meet with someone who doesn't deserve to share your air, let alone your history."

· · ·

As I lean closer, her eyes darken, and she bites her lower lip. She tries to keep up her tough facade, but I can see the flicker of surprise and maybe even delight in her gaze.

"Jealousy doesn't suit you, Guillaume," she retorts, but her voice is laced with a hint of breathlessness.

I take a step closer, my heart pounding against my chest. "Peut être," I concede, "but indifference would be a lie."

Her eyes widen as she realizes what I'm implying, and she takes a small step back. But I can't hold back any longer. "Then don't lie," she whispers as I close the remaining distance between us.

I wrap my arms around her, pulling her into a desperate embrace. "I'm not considering going back to anyone," she murmurs against my chest, sending shivers down my spine.

"I won't let you," I declare. "You're mine," I blurt out, unable to contain my possessiveness over this woman who sets my world on fire.

A spark of something ignites in her eyes at my possessive words. "Okay," she breathes, and I know then that she's mine.

• • •

"Okay," I repeat, my resolve solidifying as our lips crash together in a wild frenzy. Our tongues tangle and teeth clash in a chaotic dance of desire. At this moment, everything else fades away. All that matters is the taste of her promise on my lips and the feeling of her fingers digging into my shoulders as she stakes her own claim on me.

The need to have her, to claim her as mine surges through me with such ferocity that I wonder how I will manage to keep my composure until we reach the apartment. But I need to lay myself bare first.

"Elizabeth," my voice comes out gruffer than intended against the backdrop of the city lights. I need to tell you something ..."

"Later. Make love to me, Guillaume," she whispers, and it's all the permission I need. My mouth finds hers again, her taste intoxicating, a mix of sweet desire and the heady thrill of being truly known.

The skyline is a blur, but who needs Paris when heaven is right here in my arms?

"Mine," I growl against her skin, marking her with lips and teeth. Every touch is a claim.

"Yours," she gasps, her hands raking through my hair, anchoring me to the present, to her. My world narrows to the heat of her body wrapped around mine, the moans that slip from her lips, the way she says my name like it's a prayer.

I lift her up and carry her to the bedroom; the mattress dips beneath our weight, creaking with delighted protest. I let out a low groan as I start freeing her from her clothes, revealing the beauty that keeps me awake at night. She's perfection in every sense - the curve of her hips, the swell of her breasts, and those legs that go on forever.

"Mon Dieu, tu es magnifique," I murmur against her collarbone before taking a taste. Just a taste, then another.

My hands ravage her body, fingers tracing every curve and contour until she is left completely exposed beneath me. I take her with a primal hunger, my nails digging into her flesh as I claim her as mine. "You belong to me now," I growl as I capture her left nipple between my teeth, sucking and biting until it hardens under my tongue.

Her moans fill the room, fueling my desire even more. I plunge my hand between her thighs, feeling the heat and wetness of her pussy as I stroke and tease her. She whimpers and gasps, her eyes wide with desire and surprise at the intensity of my touch. My cock throbs with need, aching to be buried deep inside her. I spread her legs wide open to claim what's rightfully mine. Her hands are gripping my hair tightly.

· · ·

"Mine," I growl, a primal desire burning through me as I nod at her. She knows what's coming. I take my cock in hand, thick and needy, and rub it over her slick folds, relishing in the way she moans and pushes against me. The fire inside me grows hotter as my tip slides over her entrance, begging to be let in. The anticipation is unbearable, but I savor the exquisite torture.

"Hold on tight, chérie," I grunt as I finally push into her. She gasps and grips the bed sheets, her body trembling with pleasure. I slide in deeper and deeper until I am fully enveloped inside of her tight warmth.

"Be still now," I command, my voice rough with desire. "Let me take you." She gasps again, her pussy clenching around me in response, slick and hot as it releases its grip on me.

The feeling of her rushes through me like a drug. Her nails dig into my shoulders with each thug, urging me deeper inside.

"Please," she pleads, "more," her voice straining with desire as I thrust into her. Her body convulses, and I grip her hips tightly, determined to keep my cock buried within her. The sound of our skin slapping against each other echoes through the room, accompanied by the soft rustle of sheets and her moans that fill the air.

"You like that, chérie?"

• • •

"Oh, YEEEES."

The feel of her is like ambrosia, sweet and addictive. With each thrust, I sink deeper into her, possessing her, claiming her as mine in the most primal way possible.

"This pussy is mine, tu comprends?"

"Yes," she whimpers.

"No one else will touch this. Ever again."

"You are mine." I groan again, losing myself in the feel of her body moving underneath me.

"Yours."

The feeling that she's mine, forever and always, washes over in waves as I let go, pouring myself into her, pounding, slamming into her.

Afterward, we collapse into each other's embrace, racing and sweat-slick skin entwined. We stay like that for what feels like an eternity, basking in the afterglow.

"Paris... it's magical, isn't it?" She whispers, her fingers tracing circles on my chest.

• • •

I smile against her hair and nod, "Oui, chérie. It is magical with you."

I trace her jawline with my fingertips, marveling at how such a fierce woman could be so vulnerable with me. "You've turned my world upside down, " I whisper against her, my voice hoarse from exertion. "Since I met you, I've been living in a dream," I continue, my heart hammering against my ribs. "And I'm terrified of waking up."

"Is this real?" Her voice soft. Her eyes widen as she tries to process my declaration, the vulnerability behind her usual defiance. It makes me want her even more.

"More real than anything." I reach across to touch her. "I love you, Elizabeth."

"I love you too," she says. "What did you want to tell me?" Damn, she hasn't forgotten.

"I haven't been completely honest with you," I admit, feeling the weight of my next confession. She looks scared. "I'm ... I'm..., " I pause, gauging her reaction, " rich...a billionaire, actually."

There, I said it. The truth hanging between us, raw and unshielded.

· · ·

Her hand goes slack in mine. I expect shock, maybe anger, but instead, I see a flicker of awe before she quickly masks it. That's my girl – never letting anyone see her flinch.

"Does that change anything for us?" She's testing me, and I love her all the more for it.

"Nothing," I assure her firmly.

"Be my protector?" There's a challenge in her voice again, but it's softened by the tremble of emotion.

"Always," I vow, my grip tightening on her hand. And I'll spend eternity proving it to her, one heartbeat at a time.

EPILOGUE
ELIZABETH

The gallery hums with the scent of oil paint and nervous excitement. My heart races as I scan the walls, each canvas a raw piece of my soul on display. But amidst all the buzz, his piercing eyes send shivers down my spine—a touch without touch, setting my skin ablaze.

"Ma chérie," Guillaume's voice rumbled in my ear, "your art... it's like peering directly into your heart." His words, thick with his charming French accent, causing my heart to flutter even more, still.

I turn to face him, our eyes locking in an unspoken connection. The familiar jolt, that electric rush that has consumed me since he came crashing into my life five years ago, pulses between us. "Only you would see that, "I whisper, the words a delicate thread connecting us.

· · ·

He grins that alpha male confidence radiating off him like heat from the cobblestones on a hot Parisian day. "I know you," he says simply, possessively, and it's not a boast but a statement of fact.

We move through the exhibition, his hand firm at the small of my back, guiding, steering, owning. The crowd parts for us, murmurs of praise for my work a distant buzz compared to the thunderous beat of my heart. This—all of this—is because of his belief in me when I was a shadow of the woman and the artist I am now.

"Remember how you proposed?" I murmur, leaning into him. The memory is a spark that lights up the night in my mind—the Eiffel Tower looming above, his knees on the cold ground, the velvet box shaking in his hand.

"Bien sûr." He pulls me close, and I can feel the laughter in his chest. "How could I forget? You made me the happiest man under the stars."

The rain is drizzling down on the bustling streets of Paris. Our past, present, and future are all here, entwined like the streets of this city we call home. Paris, with its ever-watchful Eiffel Tower standing tall and proud against the darkening sky, has been witness to our love story, cradling it within its embrace.

I feel the warmth of his body near mine and the electricity between us. "Happy anniversary," I breathe out.

. . .

He leans in closing the space between us and kisses me hungrily, his lips tasting of champagne. "Happy anniversary," he murmurs sealing my words with a kiss that tastes of forever, a vow, a promise, a destiny fulfilled.

As we pull away, our hands find each other, our fingers intertwined like a perfect puzzle.

"Come on," he growls, sending shivers down my spine, "let's show them what true love looks like." And so we do. With every glance, touch, and laugh we share, we paint a picture more vivid than any I've ever put on canvas. I know that this man, this city, this life is my true masterpiece - one that I wouldn't trade for anything in the world.

VENETIAN WHISPERS

1

BIANCA

As the boat slows down at the dock in Venice, the city's romantic charm envelops me, and butterflies flutter in my stomach. My heart races as I step onto the cobblestone street, taking in the sights and sounds around me. Gondolas bobbing on the canal, glistening under the golden sunlight; laughter rings out from a nearby café. It's like stepping into a dream. I need to immerse myself in this fairytale world while I have the chance. But first things first: finding Gianna and get the keys to her apartment.

I stroll down narrow alleys, map in hand, trying to shake off my tiredness from the long journey. My heels click-clack against the pavement as I navigate through maze-like streets lined with pastel buildings and quaint shops selling Venetian masks and trinkets. Grabbing my attention is an old bookstore where aged tomes sit haphazardly stacked on rickety bookshelves amidst tourists browsing through them —the musty smell intoxicates my senses as I step inside. I flip through pages of ancient texts about love stories written by Casanova himself!

. . .

"How fitting," I think wryly, buying one as a souvenir before continuing on my way towards my hotel near Piazza San Marco, where centuries-old buildings stand tall like giants watching over everything below them.

My heart hammers in my chest—a wild, arrhythmic beat—as I weave through the throngs of lovers and tourists on the stone bridges of Venice. The air is thick with the scent of saltwater and the tang of rich espresso that wafts from the tiny cafes dotting the canals.

I'm lost in a city that breathes romance, my senses alive with the vivid hues of Venetian life, the azure of the sky, the blush of sunrays on ancient walls, and the bold colors of the gondoliers' striped shirts.

He appears out of nowhere, a force of nature amidst the serenity—a man whose presence sends an electric shock through the crowded calle. Blondish hair, a strong jaw as if carved by the old masters themselves, and eyes so piercing they could cut through the crowd's murmur. He locks onto me as if he's been seeking me out all along, as though we are the only two people in this labyrinthine city.

"Scusa," he murmurs, his voice a low rumble that resonates deep within me as his body brushes against mine—accidental yet fraught with a tension that feels anything but. Our eyes clash, like staring into a storm about to break. Fierce. Unyielding.

. . .

"Excuse me?" I retort, my voice betraying a tinge of defiance —even as my body betrays my sudden, inexplicable interest. I'm not one to be dominated, not by any man. Yet here, with him, there's a pull, a primal dance beginning between predator and prey.

"Mi dispiace," he says again, this time with a half-smirk that tells me he's not sorry at all. His hand grazes my arm, deliberately, sending shivers cascading down my spine. I should pull away and reclaim my space, but I don't. Instead, I stand rooted to the spot, caught in the snare of his gaze.

Venice hums around us, the lapping waters of the canal, each ripple mirroring the flutter of my pulse and this fleeting moment.

"Are you following me?" I ask, my tone playful yet edged with an underlying challenge.

"Would you like me to?" There's a promise in his words, an unspoken vow that alarms and entices me.

Heat flushes my cheeks, and I turn away, feigning nonchalance and disinterest. But even as I take a step, I feel him there, just a breath away, his possession as tangible as the historic stones beneath our feet.

. . .

"Perhaps," I whisper over my shoulder, emboldened by desire and the intoxicating spell of Venice. The word is a mere wisp of sound, but it hangs heavy between us—a sweet dare, an invitation to chase.

And, oh, how I want him to chase.

2

———————

CLARKE

The morning sunlight bathes the Venice branch of my architectural empire as I stroll through the bustling office. My eyes are hidden behind sunglasses; I savor the anonymity that allows me to roam freely. The encounter with a mysterious brunette lingers in my mind, her allure refusing to fade. I can't get her out of my head. Those deep brown eyes, full lips, curves that go on for days. I've never wanted someone so badly. As I walk into the office, I can still see her body and defiant look in my mind's eye.

Then, suddenly, there she is. Talking to Gianna at reception, a vision of grace, lustrous dark hair cascading down her shoulders. She exudes a captivating Italian charm that I find irresistible. My heartbeat quickens. I want to devour every inch of her right here.

I approach the reception area "Gianna, my dear, who is this vision gracing our humble abode today?" I ask, my eyes locked onto her.

. . .

Gianna chuckles, catching onto the playful tone. "Oh, this is my friend Bianca. She just arrived from Bari. I promised her a tour of the architectural wonders of Venice."

Bianca. Even her name is sexy.

"Clar-k, meet my friend Bianca," Gianna says.

I take her hand, reveling in the warmth of her skin. "Pleasure to meet you, Bianca."

"A journey from Bari to Venice – quite the leap! And what brings this delightful creature to our doorstep?" I continue, my gaze unwavering.

She blushes, innocent on the outside, but I know there's a vixen within. Perfect.

Gianna winks at Bianca before turning back to me. "Well, she wanted to see where I work, and who am I to deny her the pleasure of basking in the glory of your architectural genius, Mr. John-son?"

"Oh, you flatter me. But tell me, Bianca, have you ever experienced the magic of Venice before with a handsome Englishman as your guide?"

. . .

"Handsome Englishman, you say? Is that how you refer to yourself, sir?" She is smiling now. Good.

I grin. "Only on days that end in 'y.' Now, my dear Bianca, since Gianna is bound by the chains of work, how about you let me be your tour guide tomorrow? A day filled with laughter, wonder, and perhaps a dash of architectural brilliance."

Bianca laughs a melodious sound that echoes through the office. "Are you always this smooth with your words?"

I bow slightly. "Oh, it's a skill passed down through the generations of smooth-talking Englishmen. Now, will you grace me with your company tomorrow?"

Bianca glances at Gianna, who nods approvingly. "Why not? How could I resist a day of adventure?"

"Perfect." I brush a strand of hair from her face, needing to touch her. "I'll meet you alla Basilica di San Marco at nine ."

As she walks away, her hips swaying, Venice seems alive around me. The sun glints off the canal's rippling water. The domes shine in the distance. I've found the woman I'm going to claim as mine. And nothing will stand in my way.

3

BIANCA

W e meet at the Basilica di San Marco. He is already there, waiting. I can't help but feel a tinge of irony as an Englishman takes me on a tour of Venezia.

The Basilica is an impressive work of art, its golden domes sparkling in the sunlight and reflecting off the intricate mosaics covering every inch of the walls and floors. As we walk through the holy space, the figures depicted in the mosaics seem to come alive, their movements fluid and graceful.

We continue the tour with a cicchetti crawl, stopping at various bars around the Rialto market to sample different small dishes. Our first stop is for sarde in saor, sweet-sour sardines flavored with onion, raisins, and pine nuts. I take a sip of ombra to accompany the dish.

• • •

As we walk, he brushes against me, making me feel excited and nervous simultaneously. He leads me through a maze of narrow streets and bridges until we reach an imposing building.

"Questa è la Scuola Grande di San Rocco," he speaks in flawless, melodic Italian as he leads me through the grand doors. His blue eyes light up when he mentions Tintoretto's paintings covering almost every inch of the walls.

"You have to see this. It's mind-blowing!" He says as he takes my hand and eagerly leads me up a winding staircase to the main room, where a kaleidoscopic ceiling greets us. The intricate patterns and colors swirl above us, making my head spin with wonder.

"Here," he adds, picking up one of the mirrors on hand. I look at him, perplexed. "So you don't strain your neck." I nod.

Time flies by. I'm dying for him to kiss me. We stroll along the canal, the water gently lapping against the ancient stones. The scent of musk hangs heavy in the air, adding to the romantic ambiance of Venice. I can feel his gaze burning into me, and I ache for him to kiss me. When is he going to kiss me? I know he wants to. I can feel the heat emanating from his body, a living flame that ignites a fire within me.

•   •   •

Suddenly he stops and turns, "Tell me you want this," and growls low, his voice a velvet threat that sends shivers down my spine.

I stand defiantly. "I don't need to tell you anything," my voice laced with desire and rebellion.

But it's a lie. He knows it. I know it.

He steps closer, the predator to my prey, and people around us fade into a blur. All I can see is him. His intense eyes hold promises of pleasure and possession, and it's all I can do not to drown in them.

"Mine," he states with an unyielding certainty that should frighten me, but instead, it sets every nerve ending on fire.

The silence stretches between us, his hands cup my cheeks, thumbs brushing my lips. My breath hitches, anticipation coiling tight in my belly. I am wet.

"Then show me," I challenge, tilting my chin up, refusing to totally surrender yet. With a wicked smile, he leans in and captures my lips with his own. It's a kiss of conquest, fierce and demanding, leaving no room for doubt. The taste of dark chocolate and espresso lingers on his tongue as he explores my mouth, seeping into my senses and intoxicating me.

· · ·

His arm wraps around me, pressing my body tightly against his. I feel the hard lines of his muscles beneath his jacket. Every inch of him exudes dominance, from the grip of his hand in my hair to the way he devours me with this kiss.

I melt into him, letting go of any pretense of resistance. My hands grip his back, desperate to feel more of him and get closer. A moan escapes my lips, and he responds with a deep groan that reverberates through me. The world narrows down to the press of his lips, the sweep of his tongue, the commanding embrace that tells me I belong to him. As we break apart, panting, the water whispers secrets only Venice knows.

4

———

CLARKE

The last two weeks have been a whirlwind, winding through the labyrinthine streets of Venice, Bianca's hand clasped in mine, her laughter a melody blending with the lapping water and the city's salty scent. She seems to light up the entire town with her presence, and I can't help but feel consumed. I loved stealing kisses in hidden piazzas, touching under the table at dimly lit trattorias, and riding in a traghetto. I am enjoying getting to know her slowly, without the burden of my true identity. She ignites a fire in me, fierce and consuming—she's mine, every fiery strand of her being, and I'm hers, though she doesn't fully comprehend the depth of my possession yet.

Bianca is late. When she finally arrives, her mood is dark and angry.

"Darling, "I greet her lovingly.

• • •

"Don't you darling me," she yells, banging her handbag against my shoulder. "You...you bastard."

Her words cut deep, and I know she has every right to be upset. After all, I have been living a double life - keeping my true identity hidden from her. But before I can even try to explain myself, she continues."You are married!"

I am taken aback. "What? No, I'm not."

"I have met your wife," she continued."She was waiting for you at the office this morning. Elizabeth Johnson, remember her?"

"No, that is Clark Johnson's wife," I say, relieved that it isn't my secret that had been exposed. I want to tell her myself.

"You ARE Clar-k John-son," Bianca protests, confusion etched on her face.

I feel a mix of relief and guilt. "That is Clark Johnson's wife," I repeated. "Please, believe me."

"My name is spelled with an e at the end - Johnston, not Johnson," I explain patiently. "And his name is Clark with no 'e'. It's a funny quirk of the English language. It's just a mix-up."

• • •

Bianca's expression softens as she gazed into my eyes. "She was asking for you, Clar-k," she repeats, "I thought..." tears starting to well up in her eyes.

"Look at me," I plead, cupping her face. "I am single, completely unattached."

"Let me prove it to you," I growl. The suspicion in her gaze wavers slowly. Venice envelops us—a city that knows all, sees all, yet keeps secrets close to its chest.

"Please," Bianca breathes out. "At tonight's ball, you'll be my official girlfriend, and I'll introduce you to the happy couple. And after that, I'll worship every inch of your body until there's no doubt left in your mind." I have waited long enough.

"Tonight?" she repeats."The ball is only for la famiglia Rossi and their guests," she says.

"I'm sure nonna won't mind if I bring a plus one," I reply confidently.

"Nonna?" Her suspicion turns into amazement at my bold declaration.

"Wait, did you say girlfriend?"

• • •

I lean down and kiss her deeply, "My girlfriend," I murmur on her lips; she moans against me, and I feel a surge of possessiveness swell within me. All I want now is for everyone to know that she belongs to me.

5

BIANCA

The room is a furnace, and he is the flame. His hands, rough and knowing, glide over my skin, leaving tracks of fire in their wake. The Venetian air breezes through the open windows playing voyeur, its whispers echoing the frenzy of our breaths.

"I need you," I gasp, not recognizing my own voice thick with desire. It's raw and honest, stripped of all pretense. He has unwound me completely.

"I know," Clarke growls, his lips at my ear, his voice a promise that unravels any remaining restraint within me. Venice listens, the ancient walls holding secrets of lovers long gone, yet tonight, they'll guard ours.

His touch—insistent, dominant—guides me and molds me as though I am clay in his skilled hands. And I conform willingly, fiercely, because this hunger between us demands nothing less than complete surrender.

"I am going to make you mine," he asserts, a fact more than a declaration, his fingers entwining in my hair, tilting my head back to expose the column of my throat. His mouth descends, and I'm marked by his kisses, each one an indelible claim. "ALL mine."

"Yours," I breathe out, conceding in the battle I never had a chance of winning. My body arches against his, craving his weight and strength to anchor this vortex of sensation swirling within me.

Venice watches—the silent third in our tryst—the city of masks and romance mirrors our urgency, its canals reflecting the heat that radiates from our bodies.

"Look at me," Clarke commands, and I do, drowning in the stormy sea of his gaze. There's no world beyond the blue of his eyes, no reality except the power he wields over my body, coaxing it toward a precipice I'm all too eager to leap from.

I fall back onto the bed, giggling, as he hovers over me. His big hands glide over my body, lingering on my hips and waist and finally settling on my full breasts.

• • •

"I've wanted this since I first laid eyes on you," he confesses as he gives my sensitive nipples a gentle squeeze.

"A bit slow, then?" I retort, but my words are cut off as he rips open my dress and presses his warm flesh against mine. My fingernails dig into his back as I surround his waist with my legs, pulling him closer until I can feel the bulge of his arousal pressed between my thighs. He leans down to kiss the top of my breast before claiming it with his mouth until I'm moaning in pleasure.

"These puppies are all mine," he declares possessively as he runs his fingers over my nipples. Unable to resist any longer, I reach up to undo the clasp of his trousers.

He hungrily takes one of my nipples in his mouth, swirling his tongue until they are hard and begging for more attention. "Take me," I beg breathlessly as I fumble with the button on his pants.

With a sly grin, he reveals a thick, fully erect cock. I feel the heat radiating off him. "You want this, don't you?" he teases.

"Oh, wow," I say, running my fingers along his thick length. I nod eagerly, biting my lip in anticipation.

"Hands off," he commands and strips me naked. He stands before me, taking in every curve of my body with hungry eyes. His hard cock hovers over my entrance, teasing me as he sways it back and forth.

"What are you waiting for?" I beg, unable to take the torture any longer.

He opens my legs and kneels down in front of me. "I'm going to lick you first," he says, pulling my legs over his shoulders.

"Oh God," I moan as his tongue finds my sensitive clit. His fingers slide inside me, filling me up and hitting all the right spots. My hips rise and fall with each thrust of his skilled fingers. "Harder," I urge.

He obliges, adding a third finger and increasing the speed of his tongue. I can feel myself tightening around him, on the brink of orgasm, when he suddenly pulls away.

"Don't stop," I plead desperately, needing that release.

But he just smirks and stands up, his cock still throbbing with need. "Not yet," he says. "I want you to come on my cock," He stares into my eyes as he reaches for a condom, ripping open the wrapper. "Lay back."

I eagerly comply, spreading my legs and feeling his throbbing cock slide effortlessly inside me.

. . .

"You feel so fucking good," he grunts, thrusting slowly at first. But my body betrays me, my moans growing louder and more desperate for him to take me harder.

"What do you want?" he taunts, whispering in my ear and keeping up a steady rhythm of deep thrusts. I can barely think, the pleasure coursing through me, making it hard to form words.

"Harder," I manage to gasp out. "Fuck me harder." A wicked grin spreads across his face as he leans in closer. "Say my name properly this time," he demands.

I laugh, feeling free and carefree in this moment with him. "Oh God, Clark-e… fuc..ki..ng Johns-t-on, please hurry," I shout.

His grip tightens on my hips as he continues to pound into me, driving me wild with each deep thrust. "Better learn it well," he teases, reaching down to toy with my clit and sending shockwaves through me.

"Don't stop doing that," I growl, begging him now as my body tenses and quivers under his skilled touch.

. . .

The bed skids a few inches from the wall with each powerful thrust. "Are you close?" he grunts, his fingers digging into my hips as he quickens the pace.

"Yeah," I moan, my back arching off the mattress. He lifts me entirely off the bed, his body pressing against mine as he pounds into me with wild abandon. The crescendo builds, a symphony of sensation coiling within me until release shatters through. He roars triumphantly as he reaches his peak, claiming me fiercely and irrevocably.

The distant sounds of Venice drift through the window, her nocturnal serenade a soft lullaby to our spent bodies. I know—in his possession, I have found my strength, in yielding, I have won.

EPILOGUE

CLARKE

V enice is set ablaze in a fiery red, orange, and pink display as the sun sinks beneath the horizon. The sky reflects on the Grand Canal, casting an ethereal glow over the city. I stand on the balcony, watching her with a hunger that consumes me.

"Come here," I command, my voice low and possessive.

She turns towards me with a knowing smirk, her lips full and inviting – the same lips that whisper seductive promises and scream with pleasure. Her dress clings to every curve of her body, leaving little to the imagination. Our eyes meet, still sharp and alluring as they were when we first crossed paths. She knows the effect she has on me; she revels in it.

Her heels click against the marble floor as she approaches, her hips swaying in an irresistible rhythm. The air between us crackles with electricity, each step bringing her closer to me. We both know what will happen next.

"Always so demanding," she teases, her voice a sultry melody that dances over my skin.

My hands are on her before I can stop myself, pulling her flush against my chest. "You love it," I counter, voice thick with desire. My lips find the pulse at her throat, and I feel her heart racing against mine. Her taste is intoxicating, familiar yet always new, always thrilling. I devour her as if each kiss could be our last. But it never is. It has been ten years, but our passion refuses to be tamed.

"Mrs Johnston," I murmur against her lips, every word a brand searing through her flesh.

"Only for you," she breathes out as I claim her mouth with mine and my hands roam, possessing every inch they touch.

Venice watches, a silent witness to our dance of dominance and surrender. The cool breeze off the canal a stark contrast to our heat. There's no room for thought, only feeling – the overwhelming pleasure as I repeatedly stake my claim – the world narrows to just her and me and only our love exists.

MUMBAI SURPRISE

1

AMAN

The low, steady thrum of the plane's engines fills my ears as I sink into the cushioned seat of the Boeing 747 for the fourteen-hour flight from New York to Mumbai.

My thoughts are consumed by the upcoming business meetings and family obligations awaiting me in Mumbai. But above all, I dread my mother's relentless pursuit to find me a suitable bride. The memory of my last visit still haunts me - her endless parade of potential matches, each one scrutinized and rejected by me. She always reminds me with a sigh that time is running out and I need to settle down before it's too late.

"You're not getting any younger," and I can't help but feel the mounting pressure and the weight of time ticking away.

From a distance, I spot her flawless skin and flowing dark brown hair, a vision of perfection that Mother could never bring into my life. Her eyes are like deep pools, inviting me to get lost in their depths. She stops next to me, her gaze focused on her ticket as she speaks in a thick New Jersey accent. "Excuse me," she says, gesturing towards the window seat, "that's mine."

I stand up to let her through, taking in the scent of vanilla and a hint of musk from her hair. As she passes by, her coat falls open, revealing small but perfectly formed breasts peeking out from under her cashmere top. Our eyes meet for a fleeting moment, and I feel myself losing control - something I thought was impossible with my years of tantra practice - leaving me longing for more, drawn to her like a magnet to steel.

She takes a resounding breath and removes her coat, revealing a petite figure with slender arms and a perky behind. Her eyes sparkle with excitement as she settles into her seat. A mix of anticipation and nervousness plays across her face as the plane taxis down the runway. There is a vibrant energy emanating from her. Her infectious smile and bubbly demeanor defy the cabin's subdued atmosphere. Curiosity and desire get the better of me, and I initiate a conversation.

"First time to Mumbai?" I inquire, my eyes meeting hers.

Her eyes widened with genuine excitement, and she clasped her hands together. "Yes!" she exclaimed. "I'm on a journey," she says, eager and determined. "A journey to uncover my roots." With a smile, she adds, "I was adopted. It's going to be quite the adventure."

I am drawn to her zest for life, contrasting my brooding thoughts. As I extend my hand, I notice her soft skin and warm touch. "I'm Aman," I introduce myself.

"Emma," she responds, her brows furrowing in confusion as she tries to place my accent."Your accent..."

"It's residual from my university days in Oxford, England," I smile.

Throughout the flight, we chat and I can't help but notice how young and innocent she looks. When she smiles, I glimpse her pink tongue peeking through. Something about her makes me feel at ease, and I start to let my guard down. She tells me about her plans to backpack and travel while pursuing her quest. My heart sinks at her being alone in a foreign country, my country, her first time outside the USA. I can't allow that.

"I have a room at one of my hotels that you can stay in," I offer. "I insist, let me help you navigate through Indian society. It will be easier for your search."

Emma hesitates, "I couldn't possibly accept."

• • •

"You have the entire flight to think about it," I remind her with a smile. "Just let me know so I can make arrangements," and I close my eyes.

2

EMMA

My feet vibrate with the rumbling of the plane as I make my way down the narrow aisle. My palms are slick with sweat, and I can't believe I agreed to let a stranger show me around Mumbai. But those eyes—so intense, so hungry—drew me in. And everyone seem to know him. Apparently, he is very rich and famous. The flight attendants were fussing all over him for the entire flight.

How bad can he be?

I hear Aman's booming voice behind me, and my heart races. Slowly, I turn to face him. His dark eyes rake over me, and my breaths come fast and shallow. The sensual fragrance of his cologne fills my senses, radiating heat from his body as he comes closer. He looks like a God.

"You still have time to change your mind," he says reassuringly. "There's no pressure. I want to help you in any way I can."

. . .

I force a smile, trying to steady my nerves."No pressure."

We walk through the hotel's grand entrance, its facade adorned with intricate carvings and the air filled with the enticing scents of exotic flowers and spices.

Inside, sparkling chandeliers hang from high ceilings, casting a warm and inviting glow over the opulent interior. The room is no exception, fit for royalty, with a plush king-sized bed draped in silk sheets and velvet curtains cascading down the floor-to-ceiling windows. The balcony offers a stunning view of the city streets below, bustling with vibrant colors and lively activity.

As I settle into the luxurious surroundings, the subtle scent of fresh flowers and clean linens envelops me. Despite my initial fears, I can't help but feel excited for the adventures that await me in Mumbai.

The next day, the hot Mumbai sun beats down on us as we walk through the crowded streets of Colaba. I can't help but think of Aman's touch, the accidental brush of his hand against mine at the airport. It ignited a fire within me, and now I am hyper-aware of him as we navigate the crowded streets. He seemed embarrassed by the innocent touch.

"Be careful," Aman's deep voice permeates through the bustling noise of the city, and I feel a sense of safety wash over me. He guides me from a distance through the uneven cobblestones until we reach a street vendor. He orders two cups of steaming chai with practiced ease and hands one to me.

The warm, spicy aroma blends with the musky scent of his cologne, which has become my own personal addiction. I sip the bold tea, feeling its heat linger on my lips.

His eyes lock onto mine, dark and mysterious. "India is more than just a place," he says softly. "It's a feeling. Can you feel it, Emma?" His words send shivers down my spine, and I know this trip to India will be an unforgettable experience.

"Everywhere," I breathe out, a confession of more than just my sensory experience.

As the sun sets over the city, the streets come alive with bursts of vibrant colors and the intoxicating sounds of traditional Indian music. Aman leads me through the bustling streets, where the scent of spices and sizzling street food fills the air until we reach Marine Drive. The waves of the Arabian Sea crash against the shore, their silvery glimmer competing with the twinkling lights of the city skyline.

I can't help but mutter "beautiful," though my eyes are fixed on Aman as he gazes back at me with a longing that promises more. The city fades into the background as we lose ourselves in each other's gaze.

· · ·

"Nothing compares to you," his words are like gravel, rough and unsteady as if the sight of me was enough to shake his formidable composure. The proximity is electric. My heart races in rhythm with the city's chaotic energy, and I know I am in deep trouble. I want my first time to be here, with him, even if we can't be together. But he keeps his distance as if wary of the eyes that could be watching us, a careful line drawn between us.

The tension is unbearable, and the desire to be close to him is overwhelming. I step closer, aching to show how deeply I care for him. I want to touch him.

"Aman," I whisper, turning to face him fully. "I ..." raising my hand.

"Don't," he interrupts, pulling away from me with a firmness that cuts like a knife. "We can't do this. It's not appropriate here." His voice is filled with regret, which only adds to the ache in my heart.

"I-I'm sorry," I stammer, mortified by my actions, my cheeks burning with shame. Have I ruined everything?

But then Aman's gaze meets mine once again. "Let me show you more," he says, and his voice filled with longing and promise.

· · ·

I didn't imagine it, did I? A blinker of hope ignites within me, and without hesitation, I respond, "Yes," reckless or brave - I can't tell which - "Yes. Show me everything." My words hang in the air, thick with meaning and longing. I pray that he understands the double meaning behind my words.

3

AMAN

I lean against the cool metal railing of my penthouse balcony, feeling the sticky heat of Mumbai cling to my skin. The city's bustle rises in a cacophony of sounds, but my focus is on one person: Emma. My heart races with longing, but I force myself to keep a safe distance.

That first accidental touch has been playing in my mind over and over and over. Each time, I am getting more and more aroused, and it's becoming harder and harder to resist.

My desire burns fiercely as I yearn to taste her nipples, to ravage them with my mouth.

I want to trace the curves of her soft skin, coating it in oils and perfume, savoring the intoxicating scent, and driving my throbbing cock into her.

•   •   •

I am pretty sure she is a virgin. Every inch of me is consumed by the need to claim her, to brand her with my passion on our wedding night. I'll spread her tight pussy until it surrenders to my thickness, marking her as mine forever.

But before all this can happen, I must convince Mother of our union. And I will do whatever it takes to keep any hint of impropriety from reaching her ears and bringing dishonor to our family.

———

We have hit a dead end in the quest for Emma's adoption records and family history, despite days after days of searching through the dusty archives of the Historic Hindu Cremation Records and online databases like FamilySearch Historical Records Collections. As a last resort, I applied for access to her public birth records under the Right To Information Act and greased some palms to speed up the process, desperate for a breakthrough. I promised her I'd help. And now I have to tell her …

I nervously clear my throat before breaking the news as we sit across from each other. "Emma," I begin, my voice betraying my nervousness. "I found something," I say, my words nearly swept away by the roar of traffic outside.

"What is it?" she asks, her dark eyes locked onto mine, searching for the truth I'm hesitant to reveal.

· · ·

A gust of wind blows through, causing a tendril of her hair to dance across her face. With a delicate touch, she tucks it behind her ear, sending a surge of affection through me that almost knocks me off my feet.

"Your adoption. It was... it wasn't all above board." I can see the impact my words have on Emma as soon as they leave my mouth. Her posture stiffens, and her eyes widen in shock and fear.

"The truth is," I said, choosing my words carefully. "Your biological parents are still alive." She had sensed something wasn't right with her adoption but never could imagine it was this.

Emma's face is crumpled in confusion and disbelief. The truth unfurls like a dark flower, revealing the shocking reality of her past - a web of lies and deceit.

I can see the questions racing through her mind as she struggles to process this information. But there is more to tell - details that I debated leaving out, but ultimately know she deserves to know.

"There was a scandal involving your birth," I continue, my voice filled with caution. "It involved inter-caste affairs, pregnancy, and the sale of the baby."

· · ·

"Sale?!" Tears welled up in Emma's eyes as she whispers, "Everything I thought I knew about myself...it's all a lie?"

My heart clenches at her words, and I can't bear to see her in such pain. "You're not alone in this," I reassure her. "I'm here for you every step of the way."

"Emma," my voice becomes a low growl as I speak, tinged with possessiveness. "Look at me." She obeys, meeting my gaze with tear-filled eyes. "I won't let anyone hurt you ever again."

"Why?" She asks softly, searching for answers.

"Because," I reply, my voice firm and resolute. "You deserve to be protected and loved unconditionally. And that's exactly what I'll do for you."

A small smile tugs at the corners of Emma's lips, but it seems fragile and uncertain, like the paper-thin masala dosa we have shared for lunch. But I am determined to do whatever it takes to shield her from any more pain, no matter the cost. Because she deserves nothing less.

"You belong to me, and I will do anything to protect what is mine."

. . .

Emma's sobs echo through the room as she struggles to compose herself. "But...you haven't even tried to kiss me," she finally manages to choke out.

I pause, my mind racing as I try to find the right words to explain the weight of centuries-old traditions and expectations that rest upon my shoulders. "My dear Emma," I say solemnly, "I am deadly serious about you."

The intensity in my voice causes her to look up at me, tears streaming down her face. "Seriously?" she whispers, her heart pounding with hope.

"Very seriously," I declare, "I ache to hold you close," taking a step closer, "I crave every inch of your body and can't wait to claim you as my wife, worshipping you in every way imaginable."

"Wife?" Emma sniffs, her fears momentarily forgotten.

"Yes, my love. If you will have me."

4

EMMA

We are finally alone. Aman's hands clutch my waist as he pulls me close. I feel his desire and longing seeping into my very core. His warm breath against my neck and the nipping at my earlobe send tingles throughout my body. I moan softly, arching into him, wanting nothing more than to be consumed by his touch. His hand slips under my elaborate Indian wedding dress, reaching my bare skin and gently caressing my thigh. I can feel the heat radiating from his palm as it slowly moves upward towards my center.

"I want you, baby," he growls, grabbing my face with a roughness that leaves me gasping.

"I want you too," I reply, barely able to get the words out as my voice catches in my throat. "But Aman...," I trail off, "I am a ..."

. . .

"I know," he interrupts and grabs my face with both hands, pulling me in for a deep kiss that leaves me breathless. I lace my fingers into his soft hair, pulling him even closer; I can feel his hardness presses against my stomach. The sensation sends shivers down my spine, and I can't help but whimper in desperate anticipation.

"You are mine, and I am yours, beautiful," he growls. His fingers find my breasts, and I melt into him as he massages them, expertly rolling my nipples between his thumbs and forefingers. My body trembles as he continues to kiss down my jawline, pausing at that spot just below my ear that drives me wild. I gasp and moan as his wet tongue traces the sensitive skin there.

"Aman," I whimper, pressing myself closer to him.

In one swift motion, he scoops me up and carries me to the bed, where he lays me down gently. The cool silk sheets feel like heaven against my overheated skin. As he undresses me, every inch of fabric feels like a weight being lifted off my body until I am completely bare before him. He takes a moment to admire me before pouring warm oil over me, his hands massaging and caressing every inch of my skin. I arch into him as he moves lower, teasingly, brushing his fingertips over my small bush. I gasp when his fingers touch against my wetness, and I spread my legs apart, inviting him in.

His mouth presses against my inner thigh, and I pant as his tongue darts out to taste me for the first time. His hot, wet mouth teases, licks, and suckles at my folds, eliciting loud cries .

My back arches uncontrollably as his fingers joined in, gently stroking and rubbing my sensitive clit. With each flick of his tongue and touch of his fingers, I felt myself falling deeper.

He looks up at me with intense desire in his eyes, their deep brown color nearly black with arousal. "You're breathtaking when you surrender to pleasure like this," he whispers breathlessly as he continues to devour me with his mouth and hands.

He stops and slowly pours more oil into his hands as he pushes in. I gasp for breath when he adds a second, a third, and a fourth finger, filling me up and stretching me further still.

I moan as Aman thrusts his fingers in and out of me, slowly at first but then increasing the pace as his other hand massages my clit. I can feel myself getting closer and closer to the edge, begging him for release. But he takes his time, devouring every inch of my thighs with his mouth.

He teases me, pressing his hard cock against my entrance, and with one swift thrust, he fills me and I can't control the loud cry that escapes my lips. "It hurts," I gasp, feeling a mix of pain and pleasure flooding through me.

· · ·

"Relax, baby, it is just the tip," he whispers, moving slowly inside me and hitting just the right spot.

His hands glide up and down my body, expertly massaging oil into my skin. I can feel his control radiating off of him, making me ache for release. He pulls out occasionally to add more oil before resuming his slow yet intense movements, driving me wild.

Without warning, he flips me over and enters me from behind. His strong hands part my butt cheeks as he pushes into my tightness, causing a gasp to escape my lips. But the pleasure quickly overrides any discomfort.

"Take me in," he growls in my ear, his thrusts becoming harder and faster. His hand finds its way to my clit, adding even more stimulation as I explode into an intense orgasm. His release feels like lava inside me.

We collapse onto the bed, breathing heavily and Aman pulls me close to his chest, tracing soothing patterns on my back as we catch our breaths. The scent of sex and sweat fills the air, adding to the intensity of our connection.

He kisses my lips softly and whispers that this is just the beginning. "You belong to me now and forever," he declares possessively.

．　．　．

And in that moment, I know it's true – body and soul - he is my Mumbai magic.

EPILOGUE
EMMA

The bass from the live band reverberates through the marble floors, making my toes tingle in time with the pulsing beat. It's our fifth wedding anniversary, and our Mumbai penthouse is buzzing with energy and champagne bubbles. But it's not the opulence of the party that makes me giddy—it's Aman, my fiercely possessive husband, who still looks at me like I'm his entire world.

"Emma," he murmurs huskily, his deep voice sending delightful shivers down my spine even amidst the chatter of our guests.

I turn, meeting his intense gaze from across the room. Everything else fades away – the guests, the opulent decor, and the breathtaking city skyline beyond the floor-to-ceiling windows. It's just Aman, exuding that same raw power and strength that drew me to him years ago.

• • •

And there's me, still completely captivated by the man I fell in love with. My protector. The man who fought for me and our union.

I quietly excuse myself from the group of friends I had been chatting with, my footsteps guided by the soft caress of the silk sari against my legs. The atmosphere is electric as I weave through the crowded party, anticipation pulsating through my veins.

Aman meets me halfway; his imposing figure effortlessly parts the sea of people. His hand finds mine, enveloping it in a warm and familiar grasp.

"Let's go check on her," he says, leading me away from the festivities and up the grand staircase to the second floor.

Our daughter, our little miracle, is sleeping peacefully just down the hall. Tonight is about celebrating our love and the family we have created together.

Pushing open the door to her nursery, we peek inside. Moonlight spills through the window, casting a soft glow over her cherubic face.

"Five years," I whisper, leaning into Aman's muscular frame.

• • •

"Five beautiful years," he replies, pulling me closer and wrapping an arm around my waist. "And every moment with you has been an adventure, Emma."

His lips find mine in a kiss that's both familiar and exhilarating as the first time our lips met. It's a kiss that speaks of possession and an ever-deepening love.

"Happy anniversary, my heart," Aman breathes against my lips, his words laced with the same fierce possessiveness that claimed me half a decade ago.

"Happy anniversary," I reply, mirroring his desire with a sultry whisper.

With one last glance at our sleeping angel, we retreat from the nursery, hand in hand, ready to rejoin the festivities and celebrate each other, our love, and the many anniversaries yet to come.

ROMEO IN ROME

1

MARCO

I stand in the bustling kitchen of Il Sapore, my famous restaurant in Trastevere, sweat beads forming on my forehead as I prepare for the lunch rush. The room is filled with the familiar sounds and smells of a busy kitchen: the sharp sizzle of hot oil, the rhythmic chopping of fresh herbs, and the constant chatter of cooks and servers. As I toss pasta into a pot of boiling water, I can feel the heat from the stove enveloping me like a lover's embrace. My fingers dance across the cutting board, expertly slicing through ripe tomatoes and fragrant garlic. I am the maestro here, orchestrating a symphony of flavors that will delight and surprise even our harshest critics.

A group of regulars sits at the bar, enjoying an aperitivo before their meal. The door chimes, signaling the arrival of more hungry customers. I can hear the excited bustle as they settle into their seats, ready to experience the magic of authentic Italian cuisine.

· · ·

One of the servers bursts into the kitchen, calling out for me. "Chef," he says with a grin, "Someone is asking for chips and pasta Alfredo." The kitchen erupts in laughter. "Americans," we say with a chuckle.

"What should I tell them?" the server asks. Irritated, I reply, "Tell them we don't serve Alfredo here. Carbonara instead."

The kitchen is a flurry of activity as orders continue to pour in. I grab a handful of guanciale, a cured pork cheek, and toss it into a hot cast-iron pan. The meat sizzles and releases its rich, fatty aroma. Using a spoon, I skim off some of the molten liquid and set it aside for later. I combine egg yolks, grated pecorino cheese, freshly cracked black pepper, and a bit of the rendered fat from the guanciale in another bowl. This will be our savory zabaione sauce.

Meanwhile, I heat water in a large pot and gently warm pre-cooked pasta over it. As it warms, I slowly drizzle in more of the rendered fat, creating a creamy consistency without further cooking the pasta. I add the crispy guanciale just before serving for texture and flavor.

"Carbonara, to go!" I shout towards the front counter.

The door dings again, and more customers enter. One catches my eye – a curvy brunette with an air of sophistication. She sits and discreetly snaps photos of the bustling kitchen before placing her order: Saltimbocca and Carciofi alla Romana. She is hot, and my heart races, imagining her full lips wrapped around each bite. The thought alone makes me hard.

She sits in the corner booth, balances her phone on a tripod, and takes a bite of her food. But instead of savoring the flavors, she is more focused on chatting with her followers and capturing the perfect angle for her latest food vlog. Meanwhile, her plate grows cold and neglected. I can't stand these so-called "food influencers" who care more about views than enjoying their meals.

"Eat your food, woman, before it gets completely cold," I think as I watch her film and chitchat. I feel like going over and put that damn phone down, but I have no time to waste. The restaurant is full.

Later on, after service, I catch a glimpse of some of my staff huddled together by the bar, all looking at their phones. As soon as they see me approaching, they quickly disperse.

Maria's pained expression gives me a clue about what was going on. "It's a review, chef," she says with a heavy sigh. "It's not good."

I shrugged it off, knowing that negative reviews are bound to happen. But Maria insisted I take a look at this particular one.

. . .

"She has 1 million followers, Chef," she says, handing over her phone.

There it is, the American woman from earlier. Her words scorch through the screen of my phone. Unfavorable. Underwhelmed. Disappointed. Each syllable feel like a punch to my craft, my pride. As I read through the review, bitterness filled my mouth.

I clench my fists and hurl a kitchen towel across the room, seething angrily. "How dare she?" I scream. The determination to change her mind hardens my jaw as I storm out of the kitchen. I don't know why it bothers me so much, why SHE bothers me so much.

The streets of Rome are still buzzing with enchanting charm as I track her down to a small café in a quiet corner. It's the perfect combination of old-world allure and modern bustle.

Spotting her sitting at a table outside, I approach her "Scusi," I interrupt, trying to keep a playful edge in my voice despite my anger. "If you butcher my language like you butchered my food in your review, we're both in trouble."

Her head jerks up, eyes wide, cheeks flushed with surprise. She stammers something, an attempt at wit or maybe an apology—I don't care.

· · ·

"How did you find me?" she demands, her eyes narrowing as she takes me in. "Have you been following me?"

I lean in close, my breath almost mingling with hers, the electric charge of confrontation palpable between us. "You should be more cautious about what you share online, "I say, my tone challenging. "I'm Marco," I introduce myself, extending a hand not in greeting but as a challenge.

She takes it, her grip tentative but her gaze steady, "Sophia," she says, her Brooklyn accent softening the syllables of her name.

"Your Italian could use some work, Sophia," I tease, brushing my thumb against her knuckles deliberately. My comment isn't just about language - it's a subtle jab at her review that questioned my heart and art. It is personal.

She challenges me with a defiant glint in her eyes."Maybe you could teach me," she counters. Feisty. I like.

"Perhaps," I muse, "but first, you need to learn to taste, truly taste, and appreciate the flavors of Roma e Il Sapore. I promise you, by the time I'm done, you'll beg for more."

A dare hangs between us, unspoken but understood. My presence is dominant and insistent. I'm used to having my way in the kitchen and beyond. And I will use every tool in my culinary arsenal to conquer her taste buds and prove her wrong. Because when it comes to food, passion, and all that matters, I am relentless. And soon enough, I will have Sophia eating out of the palm of my hand, one way or another.

2

SOPHIA

"**M**aybe you could teach me," I stare at him, unable to resist his charm. His arrogance is unbelievable, but he is so hot.

My eyes trace the sharp angles of his face, admiring the way the sunlight dances across his olive skin. His dark hair is styled in a perfectly messy look, and his deep brown eyes hold a hint of mischief as he teases me about my Italian language skills. Growing up with Nonna, I was constantly reminded of how important it is to speak the language, but I can barely string two words together.

I am feeling guilty now for being too harsh on him during my livestream, and I am tempted by his offer of a tour of Rome's hidden gems and flavors. My viewers will surely love this off-the-beaten-track tour of Rome with an authentic Roman God as my guide. What could possibly go wrong?

. . .

"I'll pick you up for breakfast," he says as a matter of fact, taking charge.

"But I already have br…" I begin to protest.

"No hotel breakfast for you," he interrupts with a mischievous grin. "We're going for cappuccino and Maritozzi. It's tradition."

A smile tugs at my lips as I imagine sipping coffee and indulging in sweet pastries with him.

The tour begins at Bonci, a bakery near Trionfale. We stand at the counter, sipping cappuccinos and nibbling on maritozzo pastries with cream oozing from the sides. Delicious.

Marco's eyes lit up with amusement as I am about to take another bite. He reaches out and wipes a smear of cream from the corner of my mouth with his finger before sensually licking it off. I am going weak in my knees.

"Let's go," he says, taking my hand in his rough, commanding grip. We stroll from Via del Corso to Piazza del Popolo, and finally arrive at Piazza Venezia. The street is lined with stunning architectural wonders - palaces, centuries-old churches, and grand facades that speak of Rome's rich history. Marco's pace is relentless as we weave through the busy crowds, his hand tight around mine, pulling me closer to the heart of Rome. The bustling street is alive with vibrant sights and sounds; I can almost feel the city's pulse.

We make our way to a hidden door sandwiched between two weathered buildings. Marco's grip on my hand is firm and reassuring, leading me to his creation hub. As he opens the door, an intoxicating mix of aged wine and garlic greets us, wrapping us in its alluring embrace.

Inside, the world fades away, leaving only the sound of our synchronized breaths and the gentle clinking of cutlery as background music. Marco takes me to a small table and pulls out a chair, his chef's hands exuding confidence and mastery.

"Watch," he commands me, and I do, mesmerized by his skillful movements. Without a word, he prepares a beautiful spread of antipasti, each movement precise and deliberate.

"Open," he urges with a hint of dominance. I part my lips obediently as he feeds me a heavenly combination of prosciutto and burrata. The flavors explode on my tongue, sending waves of pleasure through my body. Marco's eyes never leave mine, triumphant in knowing that he has orchestrated this moment of surrender.

"Good?" His voice is low and possessive, his eyes dark and intense as they meet mine.

· · ·

"Amazing," I admit, barely able to contain the hunger he stirs in me with each bite.

"This is just the beginning," he promises with a sly grin, and I believe him. He has a plan, a map of flavors and sensations to guide us through Rome and this simmering tension between us.

As we wander through the winding streets of Rome, I feel the warmth of his palm against mine as he leads me to our next stop.

"Rome isn't just seen; it's felt," he murmurs, his voice rich and smooth like a glass of fine wine. We stop at the base of the Colosseum, the sunset radiating a golden halo around us. He pulls me close, one hand splayed at the small of my back, claiming me as his.

With gentle but possessive fingers, he twists a lock of my hair and tilts my head back. His lips descend upon mine, hot and insistent. I taste the city on his tongue, a mingling of power and history that leaves me breathless.

The kiss deepens, and I feel his teeth graze my bottom lip, marking me as his own. He devours every sound that escapes my mouth as if they are the sweetest delicacies. Rome fades away until there is only Marco and his hold on me. Our exploration has just begun, but I am already lost in the depths of this city and in him.

3

SOPHIA

I sit in the dim corner of Il Sapore, tracing patterns on the linen tablecloth with my fingernail. My stomach churns as I wait for Marco to show up. He has never been late, not once in the last ten days. I can't shake the feeling that something is wrong. My thoughts are interrupted by a sudden commotion at the entrance. I look up and see a stunning Italian woman enter the restaurant.

"Isabella," one of the staff greets her. "Buongiorno. Marco ... is not..." but she ignores him and walks past him, sashaying through the room like she owns every inch of it, her hips swinging, a predatory gleam in her eyes. I shrink into my seat. My heart sinks as she approaches me, clearly recognizing me.

"Carissima," she purrs as she approaches, malice barely concealed by the syrupy sweetness of her voice. Her smile doesn't reach her eyes as she continues, "You must be the latest ..."

· · ·

I cut her off before she can finish. "Excuse me," I interject, my voice laced with steel that surprises even me.

Isabella sneers, her perfectly manicured nails tapping against her designer handbag. "Darling, don't be so naïve," she says with mock sympathy. Her voice drips with honey-coated lies. My heart races as I try to process her words.

"What are you saying?" I ask, my voice barely above a whisper.

"He's Italian," Isabella says with a dismissive flick of her manicured nails. "He can't help but chase after pretty things, and I let him. But in the end, he always comes back to me. Only I can truly satisfy him."

I feel sick. Poison drips from her words, but doubt creeps in. No. No, it can't be.

"No, Marco loves me," I counter, my voice more a whisper than the confident declaration I intended.

"Love?" Isabella laughs, flipping her long black hair over her shoulder. "Marco doesn't know love. Only possession. You're just another plaything in his collection."

· · ·

Her accusations claw at me like sharp nails. The familiar sound of the door chimes breaks through the tense silence, and Marco steps inside. Our eyes lock—mine pleading silently for him to dispel the terror gripping me—but the storm swirling in his dark eyes doesn't reassure me.

"Isabella," he greets icily, each syllable coated in cold disdain. Guilt?

"Marco," she replies huskily, leaning in with a mocking affection as her lips graze his cheek. I feel my stomach churn with disgust.

"Leave," he growls, his words dripping with anger and warning.

Marco doesn't know love. Only possession.

Her words ring in my ears, his alpha possessiveness grating on me now.

"Make me," she challenges, her hand creeping up, grazing his arm in a move that is both too intimate and too familiar. His jaw clenches, muscles working beneath his olive skin.

"Enough," I spit out, unable to hold back any longer. Both turn to look at me, surprised by the bite in my tone.

$\cdot\ \cdot\ \cdot$

"Is this true?" I demand, my eyes fixed on Marco as I search for any sign of betrayal. "You are... together?"

"Noo," but there's a flicker in his eyes. It's subtle, but it's there—the shadow of something I can't quite decipher. Doubt and fear swirl within me. "Amore—" Marco starts, reaching out towards me.

"Don't," I warn, swatting his hand away. I stand abruptly, my chair scraping loudly against the tiled floor.

"Think about this, Sophia," Marco says.

The thought of him with another woman makes my blood boil. The idea of being the other woman makes my blood boil.

"I think we're done here," I say, my voice steady despite the tumult inside me. "Goodbye, Marco." I turn and walk away, the weight of his stare burning into my back, the sharp sting of betrayal and loss tightening my chest.

4

———

MARCO

I can't believe it. What just happened?

My hands shake as I hold my phone, trying to call Sophia. Isabella stands before the door, blocking my path with a sly smirk.

"She doesn't love you, you see?" she taunts me, enjoying my pain. "Walking out without a fight. You need passion, baby."

"Get out my way," I scream at her. "I can't believe you have the audacity to come back."

With every passing second, my anger grows until I know I need to leave before something happens. After the deceit, the lies, and the betrayal, she comes and ruins my life again. I need to speak to Sophia.

"Baby ..." a tear starts falling down her cheek.

"I'm not falling for that trick again, Isabella."

Damn, she won't get out. I walk toward my office. Isabella follows me in and closes the door. She opens her coat, and underneath just her lace bra and panties. I swallow hard against the lump in my throat, my fists clenched at my sides. This is not desire but pure anger. Finally, I know I am free from her manipulative grasp.

"Marco! Don't you want me?" She says, throwing her coat on the floor. Memories of her infidelity flood my mind, images of her in another man's arms, their bodies entwined in passion.

"No, I don't want you," I say firmly.

"You're all I think about. You're all I want. I am so sorry," she pleads with me, tears streaming down her face as she begs forgiveness.

"Get out of my life, Isabella. You're nothing but a fucking cheater and a liar."I shout, pushing her towards the door "Get the fuck out!!!"

. . .

As soon as she's gone, my heart feels like it's in my throat. I can't think, can't breathe, can't move. All I can do is pace the length of my office, my mind going over every minute I have spent with Sophia. I can't lose her. I love her. I truly love her. I need her. I crave her.

My fingers tremble as I dial her number for the tenth time. No answer. My heart races as I speed to her hotel. I burst through the lobby doors and take the stairs two at a time. My mind spins with fear.

I reach her door and bang on it, "Sophia, please," I beg, my fist hitting hard against the wood, " Open the door, I know you are there."

"Go away," she screams.

But I refuse to leave. "I won't go away," I shout, my fists pounding against the door. "And I won't stop banging at this damn door until the entire hotel has heard me."

After what feels like an eternity, the door creaks open, and Sophia's red-rimmed eyes meet mine.

Without warning, I push her against the wall and hold her there with my body, my hand tangled in her hair. I kiss her hard, my tongue demanding entry, forcing her mouth open.

She gasps and struggles, but I'm not letting up. My other hand finds the soft skin of her waist, pulling her closer still.

"I need you," I whisper between kisses, unable to keep the raw emotion from escaping me.

"No, stop," she says.

"Baby, Isabella is just a memory, Amore. You are my present and future," my fingers gently trace her jawline as I continue, "She almost ruined me for any other woman. Until I met you."

Tears glisten in her eyes as she brings up the past. She hesitates, still unsure." She said..."She starts before I cut her off.

"I love you, Amore; there is no one else for me."

"Tell me you don't want me, "I say.

"I can't," she replies.

I wrap my arms around her waist and lift her onto the bed. I want her to feel every ounce of my desire. I claim her mouth as if it's the last thing I'll ever taste. She moans, and I know she wants me just as badly. I trail kisses down her neck, nipping at her skin hard enough to leave marks. Her scent envelops me, and I groan low in my throat.

"Please," she begs, her voice trembling.

"What do you want?" I ask, my voice hoarse with need.

She bites her lip and looks down at me. "She said she's the only one who can satisfy you. Prove to me it's not true," Sophia pleads with me, her fingers clenching the sheets.

She's mine, I'm hers, and I'll prove it to her.

I yank off her clothes roughly, throwing them to the side to reveal her perfect body. I lick a line down her stomach, dipping my tongue into her navel before trailing lower. She tastes like sweet honey and sin. I bite her inner thigh before diving in between her legs. The sounds of our gasps and moans fill the room. I lick her slowly, teasingly, taking my time claiming her, wanting to watch her squirm under my mouth.

I can feel her walls contract around my tongue. She's writhing beneath me now, begging for release. I bite down on her clit, hard. She cries out, her nails digging into my scalp, her muscles tightening.

· · ·

I look up, watching her face contort in ecstasy as I continue to feast.

I hold her gaze and rise to my feet, tearing my clothes away. She watches me hungrily, her eyes tracing every muscle and curve of my body.

"Say it," I command, my voice low and demanding.

"Marco," she whispers, aching with desire. I position myself between her legs as she spreads them wide for me.

"You are mine," I growl possessively."Mia, solo mia."

She responds by wrapping her legs tightly around me and pulling me closer. Her walls contract around me, but I push in deeper, wanting to fill her completely.

"More," she moans, breathless and desperate. "I want you."

I oblige, slamming into her, moving in and out of that hot wetness hard. I will possess this woman. Body and soul.

Her nails dig into my back, her tight muscles clench around me once more, my heart beating so loudly I swear everyone can hear it.

•   •   •

"Is this what you need?" I whisper against her lips.

"Yes ... harder... fuck me harder!" she begs, her voice raw with pleasure.

"Are you sure? You don't have to do this just for me," I remind her.

"Yes, Marco," she gasps, lost in the moment. "Please..."

I take her roughly, slamming into her with a ferocity that shocks me. She cries out, clawing at my back as I continue to pound into her, owning her. I am lost in this possessive need for her.

Her taste, smell, and every sensation are branded on my brain. I can't get enough of her. I need her to scream my name.

"Look at me," I say. "Look at me," I growl, locking eyes with her as we move together. "Sophia," I whisper as she screams out my name, her voice high-pitched and broken.

I bite her neck softly as we both come together, our bodies shuddering from the intensity of it all. And suddenly, it's as if I can breathe again. My heart rate slows down; every cell in my body relaxes. It's like finding air after holding my breath for what feels like forever.

. . .

I hold her close in my arms, never wanting to let her go.

EPILOGUE
SOPHIA

The rich, savory aroma of garlic and onions wafted through the bustling kitchen of Il Sapore. Pots simmer on the stovetop, sending steam and fragrant herbs into the air. I weave through the controlled chaos; the restaurant pulses like a living heart—Marco's domain, my playground. My heels click on the tile, sharp and assertive, a rhythm that sings 'I belong.'

"Amore, table four needs your magic touch," I call out to him in a smooth, confident voice.

Marco turns, his eyes finding mine across the chaos. Despite the busy restaurant around us, we are in our own world. Heat. That look never fades, even after five years, branding me with silent possession. He nods, his focus returning to the searing pans before him, the master of his craft.

· · ·

His latest creation sits on display in the corner of the room —a fusion dish inspired by our honeymoon in Thailand. It's bold, a testament to our shared passion for pushing boundaries.

I slip into the humming dining area, the murmurs of satisfied customers wrapping around me like a well-loved shawl. I take on my role as the face of Il Sapore, sharing stories with the media and enticing customers to try Marco's unique culinary offerings. Each tweet, each post is a love letter, whispering, "Taste. Savor. Indulge."

A server brushes past, her tray laden with glistening glasses and a dessert that's sin incarnate. The rich scent of dark chocolate fills my senses, evoking a sense of pride and protectiveness. This is more than just a restaurant - it's our empire, built from sweat, dreams, and an insatiable passion.

Back in the office, I update our social media—a photo of Marco at the stove, intensity etched into every line of his face. The image screams strength, power, and his unyielding grip on the pots and my heart. Comments flood in, the public drawn to the flame of his genius, the allure of our story.

"Come here," Marco's deep, commanding voice slices through the chatter of the crowded restaurant as he stands in the doorway. I can feel the weight of his gaze on me from across the room, and anticipation prickles along my skin. I can smell his familiar cologne and a hint of sweat from his busy kitchen. He towers over me, his solid presence crowding me against the desk. His hands grasp possessively at my waist, pulling me towards him until our bodies are pressed together tightly.

"Mia," he growls, his Italian accent thick and intoxicating. "Tu sei mia."

Before I can even respond, his mouth crashes down on mine. He bites my lip with just enough force to elicit a delicious sting before pulling away with a grin. The message is clear - I am his in every way that counts. It's a passionate, possessive kiss that leaves me breathless and wanting more. This is us - entwined in each other's arms, lost in the world of Il Sapore. We're more than husband and wife; we're co-conspirators and partners in our dance of spice and heat.

NEW YORK MELODY

PROLOGUE
AVA

I weave through the crowded New York streets, dodging people and cars as I rush towards the diner. My guitar case bounces uncomfortably against my back, but I barely register the discomfort. The city's pulse is infectious, and I'm caught up in its rhythm.

I burst through the doors of the diners and tie on my apron, ignoring the familiar greetings from co-workers. Their voices fade into the background, the clanging of dishes and sizzling of grease fills my ears, but my mind is elsewhere.My fingers twitch, aching for the smooth neck of my guitar instead of this dingy notepad.

As I take orders on autopilot, my mind drifts to the gig tonight. Will anyone even show up? My dreams of making it big mock me. This isn't why I came to New York. I was meant for more than slinging burgers at some hole-in-the-wall diner.

. . .

The seconds seem drag as I count down to the end of my shift. As soon as I'm off, I bolt out the door. The promise of the stage calls me, even if it's just at a tiny club. Under the spotlight, with my guitar in hand,I feel alive. The city's energy courses through my veins. This is why I came to New York - to live and breathe in this chaotic, vibrant world where anything is possible.

I burst through the door of my cramped apartment, the scent of Lily's cooking greeting me.I drop my guitar case and flop onto the worn couch, sending a puff of dust into the air.

"How was the diner?" she asks, not looking up from the stir fry sizzling in our dented pan.

"Same old, same old," I reply with a sigh. "Burgers and small talk."

Lily gives me a sympathetic smile as she brings over two mismatched bowls. We eat perched on stools in our postage stamp-sized kitchen, knees knocking in the tight space. But I don't mind. Having Lily by my side makes this shoebox apartment feel like home.

I tell her about the new song I'm working on between bites, my fingers dancing over imaginary frets. As I describe playing another near-empty club tonight, the familiar creases on her forehead appear.

· · ·

"Your time is coming," she says, squeezing my hand. "I just know it."

I try to mirror her optimism, but doubt still grinds at me. I've been chasing this dream for so long with barely any success. But giving up isn't an option. Music is in my blood, pulsing through my veins.

Lily sees the determination in my eyes. "Come on, let's jam for a bit before your show. It'll help calm your nerves."

I follow her to the couch, where our guitars lean against each other like old friends. The city fades away as we play. This is all I need.

I lean into the music, fingers flying over the frets as I pour my longing into every note. The soaring highs and gut-wrenching lows echo my inner turmoil. This is the only place I feel truly free.

As the last chord fades, I meet Lily's shining gaze. "That was amazing!" she says. "The crowd is going to love your new song tonight."

I manage a half-hearted smile, even as my stomach twists with nerves. "I hope so. But it's hard to get excited about playing for a handful of people."

· · ·

Lily grabs my shoulders; her expression is serious. "Every show is one step closer to your dreams. You just have to keep believing."

Her unwavering faith lifts my spirits. She's right - I can't give up now. The pain of rejection is nothing compared to the regret of never trying. I pull Lily into a fierce hug. "Thank you," I whisper. "I don't know what I'd do without you."

She squeezes me tight. "That's what best friends are for. Now go out there and show the world what you've got!"

I finish getting ready, envisioning the day my music finally reaches the right ears. Soon, playing to sold-out crowds in cavernous venues. But I'll keep chasing my dreams one tiny club at a time.

Backstage, I peek at the crowd, even smaller than I expected - just a handful of people around rickety tables nursing their drinks. I take a deep breath as I step onto the cramped stage, adjusting my guitar.

1

AVA

The spotlight hits me as I walk on stage, momentarily blinding me. I blink rapidly, trying to get my bearings and take a deep breath, willing my nerves to settle. The crowd's chatter quiets to a hush as all eyes turn to me. I spot Lily standing right up front, shooting me a thumbs up. Seeing her familiar face in the sea of strangers helps calm me.

Adrenaline floods my veins.

This is it.

I strum the first chord on my Gibson acoustic, fingers dancing effortlessly over the strings. The notes ring out crisp and clear in the intimate space. As I launch into the opening verse, muscle memory takes over.

. . .

In the shadows, a striking figure watches me intently. Our eyes meet, and an electric current passes between us. He sees me - truly sees me - in a way no one has before. Heat rushes through my body as desire flares hot and urgent inside me. But I push it aside and continue to sing, hyper-aware of his piercing blue eyes tracing my every move.

I close my eyes, trying to lose myself in the music. The lyrics pour from my lips, raw and real. My voice comes out smooth and strong. I am the music; it flows through me. Eyes closed, I sway, consumed by the heady rush of performance. The crowd seems to fade away; it's just me and the song. I give it my all, holding nothing back.

The final notes fade into charged silence before sparse applause echoes through the room. After my set, I make my way to the bar, where Lily waits with open arms. "You killed it out there!" she pulls me into a quick hug, her eyes sparkling with pride and excitement.

I can feel his eyes on me from across the room, sending chills down my spine. As I return Lily's smile, my eyes lingers on him - the handsome stranger seated alone at a table in the back. Our eyes meet again, and I feel the electric jolt passing between us.

Lily notices my distraction." Who's that?" she asks, following my gaze.

• • •

"I don't know," I reply, unable to break eye contact with him. He exudes power and privilege, tall and broad-shouldered, with sharp features and an impeccable suit. But there's also a rawness in his eyes that draws me in. My breath catches when he rises from his seat and walks through the crowd towards us. He stands in front of me now, close enough that I can smell his cologne and feel the heat radiating off him.

"You were captivating." His deep baritone voice sends shudders down my spine as his hand tucks a stray hair behind my ear.

"T-thank you," I stammer out, barely able to form words under his intense stare.

"What's your name, songbird?" His lips brush against my ear.

"A-Ava," I manage to say, my voice trembling.

"Ava." He repeats my name like a caress, leaving me weak in the knee. "I'm Alex."

The sound of my name on his lips only intensifies the ache inside me. "It's nice to meet you, Alex."

• • •

"The pleasure is all mine." His eyes gleam as he leans in closer as to promise pleasure and pain in equal measure.

"Now, tell me, Ava, why have I never seen you here before?"

His question sounds casual, but there's an intensity in his gaze that demands an answer. My heart races as I struggle to form words under his dark and seductive gaze. "This is only my first night performing here."

"One of many, I hope," he says with a satisfied grin before suddenly leaving me lost in the tangle of emotions and desire he has stirred within me.

2

ALEX

My heart pounds like a war drum as she steps into the spotlight. I sit in the shadows at my usual table, my eyes never leaving her as she takes her place. This is the third night in a row that I have come to watch her perform, unable to resist her pull on me.

Each night, she reveals a little more about herself - a music student juggling part-time jobs to support her dreams of making it big someday. And each night, I am falling deeper under her spell.

My eyes gleam with hunger as they rake over her luscious body, every curve and line begging for my touch. She grips the microphone with trembling fingers, sending shivers down my spine as I imagine those same fingers wrapped around my cock.

. . .

The song ends, and I stand, my body drawn towards hers like a magnet. My desire has become too much to contain, and I make my way towards her, ready to fulfill all the fantasies she has awakened in me.

3

AVA

I step into the spotlight, my heart pounding. All eyes turn to me.

He is there again, sitting in the shadows at his usual table. Alex. I have been thinking about him for days. His ice-blue eyes gleam as they rake over my body, leaving a trail of heat in their wake.

I grip the microphone with trembling fingers, my nerves melting into desire under the intensity of his gaze. The music starts.

I sing, pouring my heart out with each note. For him. Only for him.

He leans back in his chair, a predatory smile tugging at his lips. King of the jungle, waiting to pounce. My voice trembles as I hold his gaze. His eyes promise pleasure and pain in equal measure. A delicious shiver runs down my spine.

The crowd fades away until there is only Alex. My blood pounds in time with the beat, desire pooling low in my belly. I ache for his touch, his kiss, the feel of his body claiming mine.

The song ends, and I come back to myself as applause erupts around me. The crowd tonight loves me, but only one pair of eyes matters. I stumble off the stage on trembling legs, breathless and flushed. What is this power he has over me?

He walks over and stops before me, towering over my trembling form. A smile flickers across his lips. His voice is a low rumble, stroking over my senses. "Come. Join me."

His fingers trail up my arm, leaving flames in their wake. "So, Ava, what else should I know about you?"

Every inch of me is attuned to his touch, my thoughts scattering. "There's not much to tell."

"I doubt that." His smile is slow, predatory. "A woman as captivating as you must have depths waiting to be explored."

. . .

Heat pools low in my belly at the promise in his words. "What about you?" I ask, struggling to steady my breathing. "What's your story?"

"I'm a man who gets what he wants. And right now, all I want is you."

My heart slams against his grip as arousal floods my veins. "How...forward of you," I manage, biting back a moan.

"I don't believe in wasting time." His eyes gleam with dark hunger. "Or denying myself pleasure."

"And you think I can give you pleasure?" The words come out breathless, laced with need.

A low, throaty chuckle. "Oh, I know you can, Ava. Come," he says as he holds out his hand.

An invitation? No, a command.

I hesitate for only a moment before placing my hand in his. The rough warmth of his palm sends a jolt up my arm. His fingers curl around mine, grip tightening as he leads me through the crowd. Possessive. Claiming.

. . .

I follow him blindly, gripped by a feverish need to be alone with this man. To give in to the desire written in every line of his powerful body. He pulls me into a private room and kicks the door shut behind us. I lean back against the wall, chest heaving, watching through half-lidded eyes as he stalks closer. Closer.

"Look at you," he rasps, tracing a finger down my cheek. "So beautiful. So responsive to my touch." His fingers slide into my hair and tighten, tugging my head back to expose my throat. "You're meant to be mine."

A breathless moan escapes my lips. Yes. Take me. Claim me. Make me yours.

His mouth crashes down on mine, hot and demanding. Our tongues dance as he presses me into the wall, his hard body pinning me in place. I twine my arms around his neck, clinging to him, drowning in sensation.

One hand slides down to grip my hip, pulling me tight against him. I gasp at the feel of his arousal, hard and ready. Need pounds through my veins, an aching pulse between my legs.

"I'm going to ruin you for other men," he growls against my lips. "You'll never want another after I'm done with you."

I'm already ruined. Lost. His.

. . .

A low chuckle rumbles in his chest. "So eager and willing. You really were made for me." His fingers tighten in my hair, forcing my head to the side. Then his teeth graze the sensitive skin of my neck, a hint of pain amidst the pleasure.

Marking me. Claiming his prize. I shiver in anticipation, ready to be taken, owned, entirely possessed by this man.

4

———————

ALEX

I wait in the wings, my heart swelling with pride as Ava steps onto the stage at New York's legendary jazz club, The Blue Note. She grips her guitar tightly and closes her eyes, completely lost in the music as she sings. Her voice is rich and powerful, filling the sultry interior of the club. Her performance captivates the audience, swaying and snapping their fingers along to the beat.

When she finishes her set, she rushes to me with flushed cheeks and a wide smile. "The energy in that room was electric! Did you see how they responded to me? I've never felt so alive on stage."

I brush a stray curl off her forehead, unable to contain my excitement for her. "You were absolutely magnificent up there. I'm so proud of you, Ava."

. . .

She throws her arms around me in a tight hug. "It feels like my career is finally taking off."

I hold her close, knowing that this moment is precisely what she's been working towards for years. She has no idea about all the favors I've pulled and the connections I've leveraged to make it happen. All she knows is that suddenly, people are clamoring to book her. And that's all that matters to me - seeing her happy and fulfilled. I'd do anything to help make her dreams come true.

As we step outside into the cool night air, I can't help but smile mischievously. "I know the perfect way to celebrate," I murmur, brushing my lips against her neck before leading her towards our waiting car, my hand pressed against the small of her back possessively.

The adrenaline and excitement from her performance are still coursing through her veins, sending a rosy flush to her cheeks and a sparkle to her eyes. Across the table, I can't take my eyes off her as the candlelight casts a warm glow over her delicate features. Our legs brush beneath the crisp white linen, igniting sparks of electricity between us.

I've brought her to Sappe, the hottest new French restaurant in town, determined to sweep her off her feet tonight.

"You look stunning," I say, reaching for her hand. She beams at me as our fingers intertwine.

· · ·

"Not too bad yourself, Mr. Mysterious." Her playful tone hides a hint of frustration - she wants to know more about my past. But I smoothly steer the conversation towards safer topics - our shared love for jazz, the latest exhibit at the modern art museum, and her passion for songwriting.

When I'm with Ava, all that matters is the present. Her laughter, the adorable way she scrunches her nose when she disagrees with me, the fire in her eyes when we debate music. The past is best left behind. We skip dessert and take a moonlit stroll through the sculpture garden. My arm is around her waist, pulling her close as we admire past abstract metal forms illuminated by soft ground lighting.

My mouth claims hers, hungry and demanding. I pour all my desire into that kiss, gripping her hips, branding her as mine. A soft moan escapes her lips. The rest of the world falls away.

For now, she is all that exists.

As Ava and I stroll through the park, her phone vibrates in her handbag. She quickly glances at the screen, then sighs and tucks it in. I raise an eyebrow, concerned. "Is everything alright?" I ask tentatively.

"It's just a work thing," she replies, tapping out a quick response before locking her phone again.

· · ·

"What work?" I ask, perplexed, "Who was it?" I press, trying to hide my jealousy.

"Why do you always have to know every little detail?" she snaps back, her green eyes flashing with irritation. "You always question me about meetings and new friends. It's like you don't trust me."

Her words sting, but I try to remain calm. "Ava," I say carefully. "I just want to keep you safe."

"Safe?" Ava scoffs and crosses her arms over her chest. "Or under your control?"

Her words strike me with the force of a punch to my gut. Memories flood back - my father's tight grasp on my life, demands, and expectations that I could never meet. "You think I'm trying to control you?" I ask through clenched teeth, feeling angry and vulnerable all at once.

My hand trembles as I run it through my hair, frustrated and defeated. She is right, and it hurts to admit it. My father's strict rules and constant dismissal of my dreams still haunt me. "You don't understand," I finally confess, "when you've lost everything, you hold on tightly to whatever you possess."

"You're mine, Ava. Don't forget that."

• • •

"I'm not your possession, Alex," she says firmly. "And I can't be responsible for healing your past wounds. And I won't be controlled, even by someone I..." She trails off, but the unspoken words hang heavy between us. Even by someone I love.

My heart aches at the uncertainty in her tone. I loosen my grip on her hands; my chest feels tight as I struggle to control my emotions. I want to protect our new love. I'm haunted by the fear that her rising star will eclipse us, that she'll leave me behind.

"I want to protect you ... us," I say through gritted teeth.

I open my palms in surrender. The choice is hers now - stay and fight for us, or turn and walk away. The ball is in her court now, and I hope she chooses to stay.

5

AVA

I take a deep, shuddering breath as I leave Alex behind. My skin still tingles where his hands gripped me, and his lips grazed my throat. He has this power over me and can ignite my body even if my mind rails against him.

I sink down onto the couch. This constant push and pull is exhausting. I am fighting against his need to control and possess me and my own to be independent.

I take a deep breath, close my eyes and run through the setlist. The pounding beat, the wail of the guitar, the ache in my voice as I belt out the lyrics.

But I want him to possess me. I always wanted him too. I miss him already.

. . .

My phone buzzes with an incoming text. It's him.

"Please ... can we talk?"

"Come to mine, please ... I miss you."

6

ALEX

I pace back and forth in my luxurious penthouse, the city skyline spread out before me. My hands grip tightly at my hair as I replay the argument with Ava in my mind. I can't believe how easily my insecurities got the best of me, leading to her storming out and ending things between us.

I turn towards the screensaver on my computer. It's a photo of us smiling and laughing together. I trace my finger along her face. "I won't let go of us, Ava," I whisper. "I'll do whatever it takes to show you I can be the man you deserve."

She is the one thing I can't control. And the one thing I want more than anything. I'll do whatever it takes until she's back in my arms where she belongs.

"Please ... can we talk?"

I text.

"Come to mine, please ... I miss you."

My heart races as I sit alone in my empty apartment, waiting for her reply. The silence is deafening, and every passing minute feels like an eternity. The doorbell rings, and my heart leaps.

I know it's her. Ava.

Just her presence on the other side of the door makes me quiver. I take a deep breath and open the door.

There she stands with her long hair falling over one shoulder and her eyes locked onto mine. The tension between us is palpable as we stare at each other, both hesitant to make the first move.

"Come in," I finally say, my voice husky.

She steps inside, glancing around.

"Alex..." she begins, but I cut her off. Without a word, I pull her into me, pressing her against the wall. Our bodies mold together as our lips crash in a desperate kiss. She gasps softly but kisses me back as passionately, her fingers digging into my shoulders.

· · ·

We are lost in each other, our pent-up longing and frustration pouring out in that fiery kiss. And then, without breaking contact, I lift her up and carry her upstairs into the bedroom.

I trail hot kisses down her neck and across her breasts, eliciting moans of pleasure. Her nails rake down my back.

"A-Alex," she stammers breathlessly, her eyes filling with desire and vulnerability. "What ..."

I cut her off once more, lowering my head between her thighs. She tastes so damn good. Inhaling deeply, I lick and suck at her pussy like it's all I've ever wanted, making her gasp and whimper. Her scent fills my senses, intoxicating me further.

Every sound she makes - moans and gasps - fuels my hunger for her. My hands roam up to her lace bra, unhooking it slowly to reveal perfect breasts to my starving mouth.

Her nipples harden under my tongue, and she clutches at my hair as I work my magic between her thighs. She's mine. And I'm not letting go this time.

My cock throbs in anticipation. I sink into her, filling her perfectly slick pussy with one hard thrust. She cries out in pleasure, arching beneath me. Our bodies move in sync, and her nails dig into my shoulders as she meets my pace, pushing me further into her.

Her walls clench around me at just the right moments, sending shockwaves of pleasure straight to my cock. Every thrust hits that spot just right until we cum - her scream pierces through the room. Panting heavily, we catch our breaths together.

"I need you," I confess hoarsely, kissing her forehead softly. "I can't go another day without feeling this."

Her eyes lock onto mine as she responds, "I feel it too... I feel it when I'm with you."

"I'm sorry," I whisper into her ear, "for pushing you away. But please, give me another chance."

She nods, kissing me softly on the lips. "I love you," she whispers back. And that's all I need.

7

AVA

I wake up in a daze, the sheets tangled around my legs. The room is dark and quiet except for the sound of my own heavy breathing. I call out for Alex, but there's no answer. Suddenly, I hear rustling from outside the bedroom door.

"Alex?" I call again, my heart starting to race.

The door opens, and Alex appears, grinning mischievously. "Hello there," he says. "I have a surprise for you," he says, "here," and Alex hands me a coat. "Come."

I wrap myself in the coat and follow him up the stairs, hand in hand. With each step, my heart pounds faster with excitement and anticipation. When we reach the rooftop, I gasp in wonder at the scene before me. Strings of fairy lights twinkle above us, casting a magical glow over everything. Candles flicker along the roof's edge, creating shadows dancing on the walls.

"Wow," I whisper, eyes drinking the romantic scene before me.

"This is for you," Alex whispers in my ear, his grip on my hand tightening possessively. I feel like I'm in a dream as he leads me towards a cozy nook with a blanket on the ground. We sit together and gaze up at the city skyline stretched before us.

Alex leans in, his lips grazing my earlobe. "Do you like it?" He asks huskily.

"I love it," I breathe, my heart racing as his hand reaches my thigh beneath the coat. I bite my lip to stop myself from moaning out loud as his fingers trace patterns on my naked skin.

He leans back, meeting my gaze with a smirk as he nips at my earlobe playfully. "I want more Ava," he growls, "I want it all." He reaches into his pocket and pulls out a small velvet box. "I knew from the moment I saw you that you were the missing piece of me," he murmurs against my skin.

"You've bewitched me, Ava. I'm under your spell, captivated, obsessed."

. . .

"Ava Mae," he says, his voice breaking. "Marry me."And just like that, the world stops. Tears fill my eyes. His eyes are wild, pleading.

I sob and nod, "Yes, God, yes." the words are out before I can stop them. His eyes light up with relief and happiness. He slips the ring onto my finger. It's perfect.

When did he get a ring?

"I knew the day I met you." Slowly, he kisses me. Deeply, possessively. I'm his. He's mine. I taste his lips, salty from his tears. I feel the ring on my finger.

I want this man. I need him. I belong to him. And he belongs to me.

ARTIC EMBRACE

1

ZOE

I trudge through the dense layer of freshly fallen snow, my boots sinking with each determined step. I'm pursuing the elusive Aurora Borealis, the masterpiece of nature I've promised my readers. But instead of finding the celestial dance of green and violet, I stumble upon a cabin that seems to have sprung out of nowhere, one of the many secret the Arctic keeps.

The air bites at my cheeks as I approach the solitary structure. I can almost feel the isolation radiating from its wooden walls.

My breath comes out in clouds as I circle the cabin, camera in hand, documenting the unexpected find for my blog. In my excitement, I don't see the thin wire until it's too late. A snap echoes as I trip, falling forward into the snow.

. . .

"Damn," I mutter, picking myself up. That's when I notice the camera trap, its lens glaring at me like an unblinking eye. The unexpected flash of the camera leaves me momentarily blinded, spots dancing in front of my vision like fireflies. My heart races erratically, and my tongue feels like rough sandpaper against the roof of my mouth. It has caught me, a candid shot of my fall. I stand there, half-embarrassed, half-thrilled at the spontaneity of it all. This is what adventure looks like—unpolished and raw.

A door creaks open, and a tall figure emerges. The icy winds around us seem to intensify in his presence. He is a towering man with broad shoulders and muscles clearly defined beneath his clothes. There's a ruggedness about him, a silent power that the Arctic has not tamed.

"What are you doing here?" His deep voice rumbles, anger flashing in his piercing blue eyes.

Good morning to you too.

He steps closer; his broad shoulders fill my entire field of view, commanding attention with their sheer size and strength. His sharp features and piercing blue eyes leave no room for escape. A musky and masculine scent lingers in the air, causing my senses to tingle. Tension radiates from his body, making every muscle appear to be made of steel.

"Zoe Harper," I swallow hard, trying to find my voice and introduce myself, brushing snow from my jacket.

· · ·

"You are trespassing," he states firmly.

"I, I am sorry ... I didn't mean to ... I just got a little lost," I explain, feeling small under his presence.

He studies me carefully, the muscles in his jaw tense, those blue eyes trying to read my every intention.

"I'm a travel blogger, just passing through. I'll be on my way; I mean no trouble."

The air between us thick with tension.

"The snowstorm will hit soon," he finally rumbles, squinting at the darkening sky. "You won't make it down the mountain tonight."

My eyes dart anxiously to the looming clouds above. He's right. Shit.

His hand clenches into a fist, his jaw taut with internal struggle. The Arctic offers few options, and he finally speaks with a hard edge in his voice. "You can take shelter here until the storm passes." He steps aside, motioning for me to enter his world. His gaze lingers on me, sending shivers down my spine. Despite my fear, I feel a fire ignite deep within me as I meet his intense stare head-on.

No name? Fine then mountain man...

"Thank you," I say, feeling the tension between us like an electric current.

Inside the cabin, warmth envelops me and chases away the cold. We are two strangers, circling each other in a confined space. I peel off layers of clothing, aware of his gaze following every movement. There's a claim in his eyes, a possessive flicker that alarms and excites me.

"Make yourself at home," he says, but it's clear who is in control here.

The cabin is as silent as him; the only sounds are the crackling fire and our quiet voices. The walls are lined with black and white photographs of battles, soldiers, and stunning wildlife from exotic places.

"These photos are beautiful," I say, trying to break the silence and chip away at his stoic exterior.

"Here," he responds, handing me a steaming mug of coffee, "You need to warm up."

. . .

"Are you a photographer?" I press on with my questions, curious. He nods in response. Man of many words. A small smile tugs at the corners of his mouth, rare and fleeting, as if it costs him something precious.

"I'm Zoe," I introduce myself, trying to fill the silence, extending my hand as a peace offering.

"You said," he replies dryly... Oh boy, this is going to be a long night.

"I never thought I'd end up sharing my cabin," he admits with a rough edge to his voice, as if it pains him to reveal this."I'm Ethan.," he says. "Ethan Frost."

"How appropriate," I mutter under my breath. "Neither did I," I quickly add, hoping he didn't hear me; this was definitely not part of the plan.

I should be wary of this mysterious stranger, but there is something undeniably alluring about him that draws me in like a moth to a flame. I am now at his mercy, but some reason, I can't bring myself to feel afraid.

2

———

ETHAN

The name Zoe lingers on my lips, soft as velvet. This morning, she had the startled look of a deer caught in headlights, her dark brown eyes gleaming like polished mahogany under her white woolen hat. As she removed each layer of clothing, I could barely contain myself. Anticipation made my palms sweat, and my heart race, eager to see every perfect curve of her body revealed in the base layers.

It's late, but I can't sleep. She is soundly at sleep in my bed after protesting my offer. Her blonde hair cascades in soft waves across the pillow. My pillow.

I sit at my desk, bathed in the harsh glow of my laptop screen against the dim light of my cabin. My fingers hover over the keyboard, scrolling through the day's work. But then, there she is – a candid shot amidst the frozen land-scapes of the Arctic. She's laughing, completely unguarded, with her head thrown back and eyes closed. The sight ignites something primal within me, a fierce and undeniable urge to claim her as mine.

"Mine," the thought flashes through my mind like lightning. I caress Zoe's face on the screen, and my heart races as I imagine her lips against mine, her body pressed against mine. I lean back in my chair, the creak of the wood under my weight grounding me to the moment. My breath hitches. I can still hear her laughter ringing in the stillness of the cabin.

Abruptly, the ping of an incoming email breaks the spell. Reluctantly, I click away from Zoe's image, my gut clenching at the sudden interruption. It's Jack, my ex-military comrade and friend, now a security expert. We share a past and scars.

"Expedition. High stakes. Need you." The words on the screen pull me back to a life I've been trying to leave behind.

Zoe's phone lights up. A notification pops up, I know I shouldn't snoop, but I can't resist. It's her next assignment details. I scan the details. Fourteen days. Our paths are destined to diverge in fourteen days.

Zoe has sparked a fire within me; she is an angel sent from heavens to save me from myself. My Angel. Now, I'm at war with myself.

· · ·

I want to make her mine; my fingers itch to trail across her skin, to leave my imprint on her body. But time is slipping away like grains of sand in an hourglass, with it, the chance to explore the intense connection.

"Dammit," I curse under my breath. Frustration boils inside me as I pace the small cabin, the floorboards creaking under my weight. The walls feel too close now, suffocating me with their confines for the first time.

"I can't let her go," I mutter, the truth settling like weights in my chest. I've lived for the thrill of adventure, but Zoe— she's a different kind of thrill, one that promises more than adrenaline.

My reflection in the window offering no answers, only the steely gaze of a man caught in the storm of his emotions. The silence of the Arctic night wraps around me, broken only by the thumping of my heart.

3

ZOE

The crackle of bacon greets me as I shuffle into the kitchen. Ethan stands at the stove, his broad frame filling the space as he easily flips pancakes. "Morning," he grumbles without looking up.

"Morning," I whisper back, my voice still heavy with sleep.

He nods towards the table, where a mug of steaming coffee awaits me. I take a sip and let out a contented sigh. "Breakfast is almost ready. Sleep well?"

"Like a log, " I reply with a grin. Mmmm, talkative this morning ...

I start rummaging around, searching for my phone. Ethan glances over at me curiously. "What are you looking for?" he asks.

. . .

"My phone, I can't seem to find it," I say with a frustrated sigh.

"On the table, " he says, nodding towards the small wooden table in the corner.

"Found it," I mutter as I finally locate it buried under a pile of papers. I check the screen and see yet another work assignment. In two weeks, I'll be off on my next adventure. A part of me thrills at the thought. Exploring the world and sharing it with others has always been my passion. But another part longs to stay here in Ethan's arms. I can't help but wonder how they would feel...

Ethan glances over his shoulder, meeting my gaze with his intense ice-blue eyes. "Is everything okay?"

I force a smile and nod. "New gig. I'll be heading out soon," he asks as if sensing my inner turmoil.

His jaw tightens ever so slightly before he turns back to the stove. The tension is palpable as the bacon continues to sizzle in silence.

"I was thinking... could I use your shower?" I ask hesitantly.

. . .

"Of course," he says, his voice softening slightly as he motions towards the bathroom. "Here," he says as he hands me a fresh towel. "I thought we could go on a hike. Try to photograph the lights." he continues. "If you want."

My heart leaps. "I'd love that!" The Northern Lights have been on my bucket list forever. To see them with Ethan...I can't imagine anything more magical.

I step into the warm shower, barely registering the steam as my mind is still lost dreaming of the Northern Lights. Suddenly, Ethan appears in all his naked glory. My eyes instantly drawn to his impressive size. He joins me in the shower and gently washes every inch of my body with his skilled hands. He teases me with his fingers, and I moan in pleasure.

But just as things are heating up a voice interrupts, "Are you all right in there? Breakfast is ready."

I snap back to reality, realizing it was all just a dream. So vivid...

We have breakfast in comfortable silence. The prospect of adventure together lifts my spirit. As we head out into the cold air, Ethan reaches for my hand. I glance at him in surprise, but he just gently squeezes, his calloused fingers entwine with mine, sending sparks up my arm.

· · ·

We hike up the trail, marveling at nature's beauty. Snow-capped mountains tower above us as we ascend higher. My legs burn.

Ethan points to the sky. "Look." And there they are, dancing emerald lights against the dark sky. I gasp in awe, and he pulls me closer. I gasp in awe. "It's incredible!"

But then, without warning, the wind picks up, and the snow starts swirling around us angrily. Ethan tugs me toward a nearby cave just off the path. We duck inside as howling winds block the entrance with snow. Shivering, I huddle close to Ethan. His strong arms wrap around me protectively, enveloping me in his warmth. My heart races at his touch. Slowly, the tension drains from my body.

"You are safe," Ethan whispers in my ear. His breath caresses me, sending tingles down my spine.

I nod, leaning into his muscular chest. I know it's true. The outside world fades away.

Finally, the wind dies down. Ethan brushes snow away from the entrance. The skies have cleared. The Northern Lights blaze as if to reassure us. I turn to Ethan. His piercing eyes glow with desire as he presses his lips to mine. The kiss deepens instantly. My fingers tangle in his hair as his arms crush me against him possessively. We become lost in each other under the dancing lights.

· · ·

In this wilderness with Ethan, I feel like home.

4

ZOE

The biting cold of the Arctic evening presses against the cabin windows as I sit wrapped in a thick wool blanket, my laptops glowing the sole light in the room. Ethan's shutter click echoes from outside, where he captures the stark beauty of the night. But my mind is focused on something else. Our days together are numbered, a truth that knots in my chest tighter with each passing moment. After the snowstorm, I didn't leave. He never asked me to. I can't believe it's almost time...

I type, delete, and type again. My blog post about the ethereal dance of the aurora borealis feels hollow without the mention of him, the man who's become the pulse thrumming through my veins.

A gust of frigid air swooshes through the door as it swings open; Ethan steps inside, his cheeks flushed red from the cold and snowflakes clinging to his dark, unruly hair. My heart races at the sight of him; he looks at me with those piercing blue eyes that hold a warmth that defies their icy hue.

"Zoe," he says, his voice rough and jagged like the frozen landscape outside."We need to talk."

My heart pounds against my chest as I nod, watching his restless pacing. He runs a hand through his tousled brown hair, the look on his face like a caged polar bear with too much energy and nowhere to go. Suddenly, he stops in front of me and turns to face me. My breath catches in my throat as he speaks. "It's almost Valentine's Day," he starts, and I can't help but wonder where this is going.

"Time's running out," I whisper, dread coiling inside me like a snake ready to strike.

"Damn right, it is." He takes a step closer, our bodies nearly touching. "I have a proposal."

My heart races as I wait for him to continue. "Tell me," I manage to say, my voice sounding foreign and full of anticipation.

"Work with me," he states matter-of-factly, his piercing blue eyes boring into mine. "Travel with me. Blog about our adventures."

•   •   •

The idea sends a jolt through me - excitement mingled with uncertainty. But the thought of being apart from him cuts sharper than the piercing Arctic wind. "Ethan...you're a lone wolf, how could you...possibly, "I want him to be sure.

"Stop."He steps closer, his hand tilting my chin up so our eyes meet. "I've been alone for too long. But when I look at you, I know I no longer want to be." His words send shivers through me.

I scan his rugged features, searching for any sign of hesitation or doubt, but there's none. Only certainty. And desire. A fierce possession and longing for me radiates from his stance, claiming the space around me as if it's his right.

"Think about it, Zoe," he continues. "The adventures we could have, the stories we could tell." His thumb brushes against my lower lip, sending another wave of electricity through my body.

"Wouldn't I just be in your way?" I can't help but voice my doubts, even as I am desperately drawn towards him.

"Never." The word rumbles from his chest like a growl."You'd be by my side. Where you belong. You're my angel sent from heaven to save me."

My breath hitches. It's reckless, insane even, but the longing in his eyes mirrors my own. This rugged, mountain man standing before me is claiming my future, intertwining our lives with a few simple words.

"Say yes," he urges, his tone brooking no argument.

"Yes."The word spills out without hesitation.

We're charting a course together into the unknown. And I know Ethan will be by my side no matter where we go.

5

ETHAN

"Yes," she blurts out, nodding, her breath in her throat. Did I hear it all right? She said yes to traveling with me, being by my side. Zoe, my Angel.

I crash my lips against hers, tasting her sweet, soft lips against mine. Pulling away momentarily, "I'm going to make you mine," I growl softly, before diving back in for another kiss.

"Ethan," she moans softly against my lips, "I want you so..."

Oh God, fuck fuck. "Mine," I yank her top off and toss it aside, revealing her lacy black bra underneath.

"..badly. I..I..." She whispers and arches her back towards me, silently begging for more as I trail kisses down her neck and across her collarbone.

. . .

"Mine." My fingers fumble with the button of her trousers before finally sliding them off of her legs.

"Etha..n baby..."She lays before me in just her bra and panties.

I'm lost in the sensation of her skin beneath my fingertips, the soft moans escaping her lips only fueling my desire to have her more. She's mine, and I won't let anyone else touch what's mine.

I growl low in my throat when she arches her back, pushing harder against me, begging for more. I slide my hand over her stomach and cup her breast, rolling her nipple between my thumb and forefinger, causing her to gasp. My body trembles as I tease her, and I smirk to myself, knowing I have her right where I want her. My other hand slides down to her thigh as I kneel beside the bed, fingers tracing the lacy edge of her panties. She's wet, so fucking wet for me already, and it's all I need to lose control. With one swift movement, I pull them to the side and slide a finger inside her sex, curling it around her clit.

"Zoe," I gasp, her eyes fluttering closed. She groans, pushing herself closer to me and begging for more. I watch as she tosses her hair, her neck exposed, and her throat's long, graceful line. I bite gently, marking her as mine before sliding my finger deeper inside her, claiming her in the only way I know how. She's tight, hot, and so fucking perfect. I pump my finger in and out, feeling her walls clench around me in response. I add a second, stretching her just enough before looking back into her eyes, seeing the need reflected in them.

"Want more?" I whisper, my voice rough with desire. She nods. "Say it, "I command.

"More, Ethan, I want more ..." my eyes bright with want as I brace myself against the headboard and position myself at her entrance. Slowly, I plunge inside her, filling her completely. It feels like coming home - claiming what's always been mine.

"Fuck, fuck..." She cries out, her nails digging into my shoulders as I bury myself deep within her. She is tight, but she is mine. I start moving slowly at first, building up a rhythm that has us both panting. Her feel is addictive; I can't get enough of her. I kiss her neck, sucking hard as I thrust deeper, harder, losing myself in the feeling of being one with her body.

My body slaps against hers, our skin slick with sweat as I pick up the pace. I'm lost in seeing her blonde hair fanning out across the pillow, the sounds of our breaths and moans filling the room. I growl, taking control, pushing her limits until she screams my name over and over.

"E-T-H-A-N, Ethaaaaan!!!"

. . .

"Mine," I grunt, feeling her walls clenching around me, her body shaking with pleasure. I pull out and thrust back in, harder this time, her body meeting my movement with a feral growl. I lift her hips, pushing her closer to the headboard, owning her completely. She's mine. Every inch of her.

My eyes flash with possessiveness as I feel the muscles of her pussy gripping me tightly. My name is a prayer on her lips as she comes undone around me, crying out in ecstasy. I follow soon after, emptying myself inside of her.

I roll off of her gently and lay beside her, pulling her body into mine. She's here with me, in the Arctic wilderness. She's mine; there's no mistaking it now. Her body shivers in the cold air, and I pull the blankets around us.

I run my hand through her hair softly as we both catch our breath, "Mine," I whisper against her forehead. The first speaks of the morning light flicking through the window. "Be my Valentine, "I say, my heart pounds as she nestles against my chest, "Forever?"

"Forever," she echoes, drifting to sleep in my arms.

EPILOGUE
ZOE

The frigid air bites at my cheeks, but I barely feel it as I stand in Ethan's arms. I lean against his solid chest, feeling the protective embrace of a man who has left the Arctic's solitude to claim my heart. His breath, a warm whisper against the shell of my ear, his breath hot against my skin sends shivers down my spine that has nothing to do with the sub-zero temperatures. I can't help but shudder from the overwhelming sensation of being wrapped in his love.

"Look up, Zoe," he murmurs, and I tilt my head back to gaze at the swirling colors of the Northern Lights. The sky is ablaze with greens and purples, ribbons of light dancing just for us. It's our private show, a celestial celebration of our first year together.

"It's beautiful," I whisper in awe, my words barely audible over the howling wind. It gets me each time. I can't help it. Memories...

. . .

"Not as beautiful as you, Angel ." His words are raw, stripped of any pretense. They are a truth laid bare under this eternal light show. Ethan's hands roam, claiming territory over my thick parka, and I know beneath the layers, my skin burns for him. I am his, marked by love, passion, and every look and touch he's ever given me. My body remembers each possessive caress as if it were a brand seared upon my flesh.

Ethan pulls me closer, his eyes burning into mine with a fierce intensity that matches the untamed landscape around us—a wildness that mirrors our own. We are two adventurers, bound by love and passion, explorers not just of the world but of the depths within each other.

"Happy Valentine's Day, my Angel," he whispers against my lips.

"Happy Valentine's Day to you, too," I reply, my heart overflowing.

His lips crash against mine, each kiss a promise, a reaffirmation of the connection that binds us. We stand there, wrapped in each other, the Northern Lights painting us in hues of passion. Every day with Ethan is a journey of love, fiercer than the cold winds, warmer than the sun on the snow.

. . .

"Let's make more memories," he whispers as he leads me into our cave - the very place where we shared our first kiss.

"Let's." I agree, holding me closer as if to never let me go.

This is our ever-after, and it's just beginning.

SANTORINI SUNSET

1

ALEXIA

As soon as my feet touch the dock, I am enveloped by the sea breeze. The salty air dances through my dark curls, lifting them off my shoulders. Ahead of me, Santorini rises from the water in a breathtaking display of white and blue. Villages cling to the cliffside, seemingly defying gravity.

My family surrounds me, their voices blending with the waves crashing against the shore. But I am lost in the raw beauty of this place, feeling both overwhelmed and at peace. The weather is typical February and perfect - cool and breezy.

"Alexia, keep up," my mother calls out, tugging my arm. Reluctantly, I follow her up the stone steps, unable to peel my eyes away from the stunning views of blue domes and striking red volcanic rock. This island feels like a world frozen in time, with a mythical aura that hangs in the air.

• • •

We wind through narrow, white-washed streets, inhaling the scent of olive trees and oregano. I can't resist trailing my hand along the sun-warmed walls as we pass by. Our path crosses that of an old woman dressed in traditional black attire, her rosary beads clicking. She eyes me sharply, and my cheeks flush under her judgmental gaze. Greek, but not quite Greek enough...

Our villa is tucked against the cliffside, with views of the caldera framed in each window. I step out onto the terrace, leaning against the railing. The deep blue sea stretches before me, deep azure under the cloudless sky. In the distance, a sleek yacht cuts across the waves.

"It's beautiful," I whisper, my voice lost in the wind that whips my hair across my face. I sense adventures awaiting me here, passions I've only read about.

I smile slowly. I intend to embrace them all. Santorini rises before me, a crescent of white houses and blue-domed churches clinging to the cliffs. This sleeping giant is slumbering beneath the Aegean Sea. My heart races, keeping time with the crash of waves hundreds of feet below.

I've dreamt of this moment, seeing the island where my Γιαγιά grew up, a place she has told me stories about since I was a child. But nothing can compare to actually standing here, feeling the wildness and untamed beauty unfurling at my feet. I blink back tears.

• • •

Γιαγιά squeezes my hand, and I can feel her paper-thin skin and fragile bones.

Her voice is soft but full of love as she calls me "Κούκλα μου," my doll.

I cling to her, overcome. She pats my back with her frail hand. At eighty-two, she moves slower than she used to, but her eyes still sparkle like the water, and her smile hasn't dimmed.

"Welcome home," she whispers.

Home. A place I've never been, yet I feel like I belong. This island calls for something deep inside me. Like a long-lost piece of my soul has been waiting here.

Γιαγιά chuckles, reading my thoughts. "You have the heart of a Greek, Alexia mou. Passionate, loyal, a little stubborn." She winks playfully at me. "Santorini recognizes one of its own."

I can't stop grinning, unable to find the words to express what I'm feeling. We stand together for a while, the wind gently caressing our skin as we take in the breathtaking beauty around us. It's a perfect moment, one that I will always hold close to my heart.

2

NIKOS

I stand on the deck of my yacht, feeling the sun's rays sear through my cashmere sweater, the Aegean breeze tousle my short, salt-streaked hair. The island lies ahead, a stunning oasis in the shimmering sea. This is my domain, my kingdom.

I expertly berth the yacht to the dock and disembark when I see her sitting on a restaurant terrace with her family. My restaurant. Her golden skin glistens under the warm sun, and her dark hair cascades down her back in smooth waves, framing her slender shoulders. And those eyes...a mesmerizing green that reminds me of the sparkling sea on a sunny day. They meet mine, widening slightly before a smile curves her plush pink lips.

Desire stirs within me as I take in her curvaceous form, those slender legs and round behind just begging to be claimed.

. . .

I can't resist. I'm moving before I realize it, drawn to her like iron to a magnet. I make my way towards her like a man possessed, ignoring the stares of others around her. It surprises me. It has been years since my divorce. Years of celibacy, despite my reputation and the rumor mill. Despite the flock of women throwing themselves at me.

I move closer, catching the scent of her perfume. Sweet, but with an undertone of spice. Up close, she's even more exquisite, radiant, and fresh as a spring morning.

I resist the urge to run my fingers through her hair, to feel the softness of her skin. She looks at me, and I feel satisfied as a rosy blush spreads across her cheeks. The invitation in her parted lips only intensifies my desire. She seems shy, like an innocent lamb who has wandered into the lion's den. I'll enjoy coaxing her out of her shell.

"What is a lovely little nymph like you doing here?" I purr, leaning in close.

She blushes even more, avoiding my gaze with those jewel-bright eyes. "Just a family vacation. I'm Alexia," she says softly. Her voice is melodic, stirring things best left dormant.

A beautiful name for an even more beautiful girl," I murmur. She is still a girl. Still, "I'm Nikos. Welcome to my modest abode." I gesture. For the first time, I feel the need to impress someone. Her.

. . .

Her lips part in a small 'o' of surprise, eyes darting to take in my expensive clothes and watch. Yes, little one. I'm no mere islander. I'm a man of power and means.

From the corner of my eye, I see her family frowning, shooting me suspicious looks. They want to protect their innocent girl from the big, bad wolf. Little do they know I have no intention of letting her go.

"I'd be honored to show you around the island if you'll let me," I say, holding my hand in invitation. Her eyes widen, lips parting again. In the distance, her fretful relatives are calling. But I am not done with her yet.

"Come back later, Alexia," I say, my voice low and commanding. "I'll show you wonders you've never dreamed of."

She turns and rushes back to her concerned family, but we both know she will return. And when she does, I will finally claim what is mine. I smile, triumph, and desire surging hotly through my veins. This island is my domain. And no exquisite treasure washes up on my shores without becoming the property of Nikos Kiriakos.

For the first time in years, I feel alive.

3

ALEXIA

As I return to the table where my family is gathered my head spins, and my body feels hot. My legs wobble under me, and I feel a dampness in my underwear. Nikos. A real man, not like the boys back in Philly. A sheer, raw animal power calling for something deep inside me, a wildness I've never felt before.

My mother gives me a disapproving look as soon as I sit down and the aunties start gossiping about his notorious reputation as a billionaire playboy. "He is divorced, ... has a different woman every week ... blah blah blah.Nikos Kiriakos, the billionaire who owns half of Santorini... stay away from him... blah blah blah...

The more they talk, the more intrigued I become. Nikos. Even his name feels hot on my lips.

. . .

Hours pass, and all I can think about is his offer to show me around the island. I didn't answer him right away; I wanted to play it cool. I wanted it, though ...

Finally, in the afternoon, I sneak away from my family. I walk down the marina, looking, hoping ...

Just as I start to give up, I hear his deep baritone voice behind me. "You are back," he says with a knowing smile. He knew I would.

"I was wondering if the offer still stands," I ask.

"Of course, my little nymph," he says with a smile that reveals straight, bright teeth against his dark olive skin. "I'll be your private guide to a world of pleasure," he says. Oh God, I feel weak at the knees already.

I nod eagerly, crossing my fingers in hopes that he means much more than just the sights of Santorini.

In the following days, Nikos leads me through the island's lesser-known parts, his hand possessively entwined with mine. We wander through the quaint streets of Oia, Fira, and Imerovigli. The winter season offers a peaceful charm, absent of the bustling crowds that flood these alleyways in the summer.

· · ·

One evening, we make our way up to the top of Akrotiri Lighthouse just as the sun begins to set, the clear blue sky transforming into shades of orange and pink. Nikos pulls me closer, his arm securely wrapped around my waist. The chilly air touches my exposed skin, but his warm breath against my neck makes me feel warm.

Every day is filled with exciting adventures: exploring the ancient ruins of Akrotiri, wandering through the Museum of Prehistoric Thera, and admiring the exhibits at the Maritime Museum of Oia. And each day, I hope Nikos finally kisses me and claims me as his own. I can't help but wonder why he has yet to make a move. I catch glimpses of his aroused state - the bulge in his trousers gives it away - but he resists acting on it. My vacation is ending soon. I want him to be my first.

After a peaceful day touring the island's picturesque vineyards and indulging in a private wine-tasting experience, he leads me to a secluded candlelit dinner. The warm fragrance of Greek herbs and rosemary fills the air as we enter a small cave with stark black walls. He guides me to a low table adorned with a crimson red tablecloth, and I sink into the plush pillows scattered around it. We are alone.

As he hovers over me, his body radiates heat, and his eyes smolder with desire. He feeds me chunks of salty feta cheese by hand, each touch sending electric shockwaves through my body. With every dirty word he whispers in my ear, my heart races with anticipation. Hopefully, tonight ...

· · ·

My breath catches as he leans in, his lips ghosting over my earlobe. His stubble grazes against my skin. One kiss from him is all it takes for my need to consume me. His kisses are intense and claiming, his teeth gently grazing against my bottom lip before his thumb traces its curve. A low growl rumbles in his throat as his fingers slip between my legs, finding me already wet and ready for him. He teases me with slow strokes and circles, causing pleasure to course through every inch of my body.

"Naughty girl," he growls, making me whimper in response.

My neck arches as his teeth graze across it, eliciting more moans from me. "Nikos..." I whisper desperately, longing for him to fully possess me.

4

NIKOS

"Thank you for showing me all these hidden gems, Nikos," she breathes out, a small smile tugging at her lips.

"My pleasure," I reply, my voice rough with desire.

Baby, my little nymph, you have no idea how much I've been wanting to get lost in the narrow alleys with you, only us. It's been a week since you arrived, and every moment spent together has only intensified my hunger for you.

Her scent—a mix of sweet vanilla and the salty sea air—drives me crazy.

"Nikos," she whispers, eyes closed. I lean in, brushing my lips against hers, feeling the warmth of her breath on my skin. She tastes like wine and sweet honey from the meal we just shared. I deepen the kiss, our tongues dancing together. I trail kisses down her jawline to the neck, nipping and sucking gently. It's like strawberries under my tongue, and I can't get enough. My hand slides down to cup her ass, squeezing gently and then her thigh. I feel the heat radiating through the lace of her panties. My fingers brush against her wetness, and she gasps.

"You're wet for me," I growl against her ear, "You want me."

She nods eagerly, moaning my name. "Nikos ...." she sighs, "I'm ... a virgin."

Fuck fuck fuck, I knew it. The thought of being the first and only one is exhilarating and intoxicating. So fucking sexy. My cock twitches in anticipation, craving the tight heat of her body. I can't wait any longer.

Pushing my chair back from the table, I pull Alexia into my lap. I kiss her deeply, cradling her head with one hand as my other hand roams over her body - tracing her spine and dipping into the curve of her cleavage. In my possessiveness, I am rough with her; she is mine for the taking.

Breaking the kiss, I look into her eyes and see the same desire reflected back at me. "I can't promise to be gentle, Alexia," I whisper against her lips before relenting to my hunger. She nods.

• • •

I undo my belt and unbutton my pants, freeing my cock from its confines. Her eyes widen when she sees how hard I am for her. She wraps her hands around me, stroking gently, and I groan.

"Naughty girl ... On the table," I command, my voice husky. Alexia complies without hesitation, and I lean her against it, spreading her legs wide as she presses her lower body against my erection. With a swift movement, I tug her panties down her legs and throw them across the room. Kissing a trail down her neck, I nip at her ear lobe, making her shiver.

"You're so fucking beautiful," I mutter, my voice rough. Hiking up her dress, I tear it off her body, revealing the white lace of her bra and her perfect breasts. Her nipples are hard, begging for my tongue. I kiss my way down her stomach, taking a moment to trace each rib with my tongue before reaching my goal.

Alexia cries out as I take her nipple into my mouth, sucking hard, tugging gently. Using my other hand, I part her folds, tasting her for the first time. She tastes like heaven.

"So fucking good," I murmur against her wetness. My fingers dip inside her, finding her entrance, and I groan as she's tight and warm around my fingertips.

"Nikos," she moans when my tongue swirls around her clit, and I chuckle.

. . .

"I'm going to fuck you now, baby," I say, sounding harsh. "Are you ready for me?" I ask as I line up my cock at her entrance, watching as I push inside.

"Yes," she cries out, eyes closed. I enter her slowly, trying to savor this moment. She's tight but so fucking hot around me.

"It hurts," she moans.

"Relax." I feel her inner walls grip me tightly, and I repeat the motion, lodging myself further inside as she gasps. "That's it, baby. Take me."

"Ni-ii-kos!!!"

"That's it, baby, say my name!!!" I growl, pounding into her, claiming her body. She nods frantically as I take her harder and faster, loving the feeling of being inside of her. I lean in and capture one of her tits in my mouth, sucking on the nipple hard, feeling her body tense and shiver beneath me. I pull back to look at her face. "That's it, baby," I murmur against her skin.

"N-N-IKOOOS!!! So good," she pants, "Nikos ... more."

. . .

And I give it to her, thrusting in and out of that sweet heat, claiming her body as my own. Her walls clench around me, milking my cock. My hands grip her hips firmly, and her nails dig into my shoulders as I take what I have been waiting for far too long.

"You ... you're all mine," Alexia's head falls back onto the table, and she arches her back with every thrust. I pound into her harder and harder. She cries out and moans, her head thrown back, and I know this isn't right, but I don't care. She's mine forever now, and I'll keep claiming her in any way I can.

5

ALEXIA

I slip silently through the ornate iron gate of the villa, my body humming with a delicious soreness. Nikos was insatiable last night, his hands and lips leaving their mark all over me as he ravished me repeatedly until I lost count of the intense orgasms that ripped through my body.

The front door creaks open, revealing my mother standing there with her arms crossed tightly over her chest, her eyes blazing with fury."Where have you been all night?" she demands, accusatory.

I gulp nervously, feeling the heat flood my cheeks as I try to come up with a plausible lie. I can't tell her the truth about where I've been and what I've been doing.

"Out..." I stammer, unable to meet her piercing gaze.

. . .

"Don't lie to me, Alexia," she snaps, stepping closer and pointing an accusing finger at me.

"I know exactly where you've been and with whom." Her eyes narrow as she continues, "That man is twice your age; he only wants you for sex. Can't you see that?" The weight of her disappointment and disapproval hangs heavy in the air between us.

Tears prick at the corners of my eyes as her harsh words slice through me like a knife. Nikos has never said he loves me; I know he wants me more than anything, yet doubt…

"Leave me alone," I shout and run into my room, slamming the door behind me with a resounding thud. The walls seem to close in on me as I pace back and forth, trying to calm my racing heart. But who am I kidding? I'm leaving in just a few days, and he knows it. To him, I am a plaything, a temporary distraction.

I race down to the beach house, my heart pounding. A feeling of desperation and longing washes over me as I knock on the door, barely able to catch my breath. Nikos answers the door wearing nothing but boxer shorts, his muscular frame glistening with sweat.

"Here you are?" he says, surprised by my sudden arrival. "Why did you leave this morning without saying goodbye?"

• • •

"I...I..." My words falter as I struggle to find the courage to confront him. Fists clenched at my sides, I finally blurt out the question that haunts me. "Do you even care about me at all?"

"What the heck? Where is all this coming from?" Nikos replies, taken aback by my outburst. "Baby," he continues, his intense gaze burning into mine, "I told you - you're mine now."

"That was just sex," I reply, trying to push away the emotions stirring inside of me. "People say anything during sex..."

"Not me. You are my woman now," he interrupts firmly, closing the distance between us. "You are my everything from the moment I first saw you - a little nymph bringing magic into my life."

"Be my forever Valentine. Marry me," he pleads, catching me off guard.

My breath hitches at his unexpected proposal. Did I hear him right? "What?"I ask incredulously.

"Be my wife," Nikos repeats. "You're the only one for me, now and forever. Did you really think I would let you go?" And then he scoops me in his arms and claims me again as his own.

EPILOGUE
ALEXIA

The antique clock on the mantle chimes seven as Nikos's strong arms wrap around me from behind. His breath is hot against my neck as he nuzzles into me, his stubble scratching my skin.

"Ten years today, my love," he rumbles, his voice a deep timbre that thrums through me.

I sigh and melt back against him, tilting my head to bare more of my throat. An invitation. A submission. His lips graze my pulse point, teasing. Testing.

"So long, and yet not nearly long enough," he continues, his large hands splaying across my stomach, possessive even after all this time. "You are still the only woman who sets my blood on fire."

. . .

My breath hitches as those skillful fingers drift lower, tracing the waistband of my dress. I ache for him, ready to be consumed. To be claimed again.

Nikos turns me in his arms, his dark gaze smoldering. "No other has ever compared to you, my nymph. My heart. My everything."

His mouth crashes down on mine before I can respond, fierce and demanding. I open for him eagerly, my hands fisting in his shirt, urging him closer. He breaks the kiss with a groan, resting his forehead against mine as we pant into each other's mouths.

"We have guests waiting," I whisper half-heartedly, even as my body sings for more of his touch.

Nikos smirks, nipping at my lower lip. "They can wait a few minutes longer. Right now, I need to feel my wife wrapped around me."

His kiss silences any further protest as he backs me toward the bed. In this moment, nothing else matters but our passion and the Santorini sunset.

HAVANA HEAT

1

EMMA

The sultry Havana air wraps around me like a lover's caress, the city's heartbeat syncing with my own. I crave its rhythm, the pulse of life that thrum through the cobbled streets and vibrant facades.

"Capture me," Havana whispers on the breeze, her voice a siren's call that beckons me further into her embrace. With every click I peel back layers of my soul I never knew existed. The colors, the faces, the laughter are freedom in its purest form, a seduction of the senses that leaves me yearning for more.

I am hungry—starved for the untamed moments that only a city like this can offer. My lens is my weapon, shield, and confidante as they catch glimpses of the forbidden, the hidden, and the unspoken desires that pulse beneath the surface.

· · ·

"Show me your secrets," I command, my finger teasing the camera's trigger with every stolen snapshot. The forbidden fruit of adventure dangles before me, ripe for the taking, and I want to devour it without remorse.

My heart races, anticipation licking at my skin with each step through the labyrinthine alleys. I live for this: the chase, the discovery, the conquest of capturing a world unknown. And here, in the arms of Havana, my canvas, a riot of life waiting to be immortalized through my eyes.

"Find something real," I demand of myself, pushing boundaries that once felt unbreakable. I won't leave until I have it all. Every hidden alleyway, whispered secret, and pulse of desire that throbs through this city's veins.

"Take me," I breathe, surrendering to the call of the wild, the hunger for experiences that would sear themselves into my memory, forever etched in the annals of my journey. Today, Havana is mine, and I—unyielding, insatiable—am hers.

The night's heat wraps around me like a lover's embrace, the scent of sweat and rum heavy in the air. My heart pounds with the salsa rhythm as I step into a club, the dim lights casting shadows that flicker with every sway of hips and turn of bodies. The music pulses through the floorboards, seducing my feet to move, to step into the world where passion reigns supreme.

. . .

Couples twined together on the dance floor, their movements a language of desire spoken without words. The thrumming bass matches the beat of my own yearning, the need for something raw and untamed. I move among them, an outsider craving to be part of this intoxicating tapestry woven from rhythm and skin.

A figure appears, commanding attention with every confident step. He moves through the space with a fiery energy that radiates from within him. His dark eyes hold an intense gaze that cuts through my tourist facade and delves into the depths of my soul.

The connection is electric, a current that zings through the charged atmosphere, igniting every nerve ending in my body, a promise of pleasure and abandonment. I have been searching for this—the raw edge of life, the dance of danger and desire.

But as emotions swirl inside me, overwhelming and unfamiliar, I feel like I'm drowning. Gasping for air, I know I must leave before I am swept away.

The sticky air clings to my skin, wrapping around me like a heavy blanket as I wander the bustling streets of Havana. My camera hangs heavily from my neck, capturing the city's vibrant pulse in every shot. Every click of the shutter captures another secret, another story, but none as compelling as him.

· · ·

I can't shake him off, Alejandro. His dark eyes have burned into mine, sparking a flame now throbbing in my chest. I can't stay away.

My pulse quickens with every step towards the dance club, the pulse of music growing louder. I can feel the thrum of desire awakening within me, a hunger for something raw and uncharted.

The neon sign flickers above the entrance, casting a sultry glow that beckons me closer. I push through the door, and the swell of Latin beats washes over me, a tidal wave of sound and sensation. The place is alive, bodies entwined in a mass of movement, a sensual display of longing and release.

I move through the crowd, searching. And then I see him. Alejandro. A vision of masculine grace on the dance floor, his body a weapon of seduction. His hips sway with a confidence that commands attention, the lines of his muscles flexing under the thin fabric of his shirt.

Our eyes meet across the room, an electric charge connecting us instantly. The world falls away, leaving only the intensity of his gaze holding me captive. He is the flame, and I am the moth drawn helplessly toward him. I know I am about to plunge into an abyss of pleasure with no intention of ever looking back.

2

ALEJANDRO

S weat clings to my skin like a sultry whisper, the humid Havana air wrapping around me as tightly.

"¡Alejandro! You are up, mi hermano," Carlos urges from the shadows. Music beats in time with my heart. Every step an assertion of freedom—a rebellion against the legacy that tries to claim me. The club is dimly lit, a sanctuary where my body can speak the language it knows best—the language of dance.

The vibrant colors of dresses whirl around me as I make my way to the dance floor. My body begins to sway in time with the music, my hips taking on a life of their own. With each spin and step, I am no longer ¡Alejandro García, son of a man who deals in darkness, heir to an empire. Here, I am fire and light, my movements telling a story only under-stood by those fluent in the language of dance.

. . .

My shirt clings to me as I continue to move with reckless abandon, outlining each muscle honed by nights of feverish dance. A sheen of sweat glisten on my brow, the heat inside me rising with the crescendo of trumpets and drums. Every twist, every turn is a declaration—I will not be the man my family demands.

Women watch me from the sidelines, their eyes smoldering with desire and silent invitations. But none can pierce through my shield. Until yesterday when she walked in—a vision that stirred a primal hunger within me, a longing to possess and be possessed in equal measure.

"¿Quién es Ella?" the beats become my heartbeat.

But there was no answer, only the call of the dance floor, the magnetic pull towards a life of my own making, defying the bloodline that seeks to chain me—one step, one beat at a time.

The pounding drums propel my body tonight as I swivel my hips, the rhythm coursing through my veins. My muscles contract and release in perfect synchronicity. My hips sway, and my feet glide in perfect rhythm. The crowd fades away, and there is only me and the music—my partner in this passionate dance. This is my escape, my passion - where I come alive.

The final beats of the song reverberate through the air as I strike a pose, chest heaving, sweat glistening on my skin.

The audience erupts into thunderous applause, but I barely hear it, adrenaline still coursing through my veins.

As I make my way offstage, I see her again. A flash of golden hair and wide eyes taking in the sights. She's a tourist, an outsider, yet her joyful spirit calls to me. She raises her camera, ready to capture Havana's essence.

I'm drawn to her, a moth to a flame. I want her to capture me. I want to know her story, to immerse myself in the adventure reflected in her eyes.

My body moves toward her, unable to resist the magnetic pull. I flow through the crowd, my steps matching the frenetic beat pounding in my head. I'm close enough now to see the rapid rise and fall of her perfectly formed breasts, to catch her scent—sweet and intoxicating.

She turns, and our eyes lock. Her lips part slightly, and a rosy blush blooms on her cheeks. My hips sway to the sultry beat still pounding through my veins. With slow, deliberate steps, I close the distance between us. Her lips part slightly, her rapid breaths matching the tempo of my approach. The space between us crackles with electricity. I cannot resist this siren call: she stirs something primal within me that demands to be unleashed. I know she is the one.

The band is playing another song. I extend my hand, palm up, in silent invitation.

. . .

"I...I can't dance," she whispers.

"Follow my lead, " I say firmly. After a breathless moment, her delicate fingers slide into mine, the contact igniting a spark that travels through my every nerve. Yes.

Without a word, I sweep her into my embrace, our bodies melding seamlessly together. The rest of the crowd shrinks into the background until only she exists. My world narrows down to the soft skin under my hands and the intoxicating scent of her hair. I'm drunk on her, addicted after just one taste.

I guide her into the dance. She follows my every cue gracefully and sensuously. The sway of her hips matches each twist and dip flawlessly, as though we've danced this dance a thousand times before. We are one with the music now, my hands roaming possessively as our hips grind in perfect rhythm. She gasps and arches into me.

"My n-a ..." she murmurs.

"Shhh, sweet girl, feel the music," I interrupt.

This goddess was made for me, created solely for my delight. I slide my hand up the smooth skin of her back, fingers tangling in her golden tresses. A soft gasp escapes her lips at the contact. The sound sends heat coursing through my veins. I pull her tighter against me, our hips undulating together. The sweet friction makes me ache with need. This vixen has awoken something primal inside me, an all-consuming need to possess and worship every inch of her.

For now, she is mine in this dance.

The music ends, and I let her go, emerald eyes dark with longing. Her cheeks are flushed, lips begging to be kissed.

"What's your name?" My voice is low, rough with need.

"Emma." Her whisper caresses my skin.

"Emma," I repeat her name like a prayer, the syllables dripping from my tongue as I trace my thumb along her bottom lip.

A smile curves her lips. She doesn't resist as I take her mouth in a burning kiss. She has captured me, body and soul. Our tongues dance together as the kiss deepens, greedy and demanding. My body burns for her, aching to feel every inch of her silken skin.

• • •

"Tomorrow, "I say, "Come and find me," and then I breaking away. I will ruin her for any other man. I will make her crave my touch, and long for the sweet torment only I can provide. She will cry out for me. Tomorrow ...

3

EMMA

"Tomorrow, Emma. Find me." And with that, he released me, disappearing into the crowd before I could protest, leaving me standing alone, my body still humming with the echo of his touch and the uncertainty of tomorrow.

The heat of the Havana sun is no match for the fire burning in my veins as I walk through the vibrant streets. Every step echoes Alejandro's last words, a cadence that propels me with urgency.

"Find me," he said. And nothing can stop me from doing just that.

My skin still tingles from where his hands have held me, and my pulse quickens at the memory of his body pressed against mine. The city thrums around me, but it is all a blur

—a mere backdrop to the vivid image of Alejandro etched into my mind.

I enter the dance club, the air heavy with the rum scent. My breath catches as I scan the empty room, searching for the man who has promised me more without saying a word. Workers are hustling. The rhythm of the salsa music pulses like a second heartbeat, urging me. And there he is, like a mirage made flesh. His gaze is locked on mine, intense and unyielding.

"Emma," he breathes as I approach, and the sound of my name on his lips is both a caress and a claim.

"Here I am," I reply, my voice steady even as my insides quiver.

Without another word, Alejandro reaches for me, his hands firm on my waist as he pulls me into his world of movement and passion. The beat of the music is relentless, matching the pulse of desire that courses through me. With every turn, every dip, Alejandro guides me, controls me, and I surrender to the dance, to him.

I want this, want him, in a way that defies reason or caution.

.   .   .

"I will show you pleasures you've never known," he growls against my ear, and the possessive edge of his voice sends shivers down my spine.

"Show me," I urge, reckless and hungry for whatever sweet sin he offers.

"Follow me," he says as the song ends, his voice a command that tolerates no argument. I follow with a delicious ache that promises everything I crave. He guides me towards the busy street, his large hand holding mine possessively as we weave through the people.

The smell of sweat and spices fills the air, horns honked, and vibrant colors surround us as we step onto the cobblestone street. The sun is high in the sky, beating down on our skin. I can feel the heat between my legs, threatening to consume me. I have never felt such a need, and it scares me.

Alejandro leads me down a closed alley, our footsteps echoing against the concrete walls. Colorful graffiti covers the old cars parked haphazardly along the way. He pulls me closer, his lips crashing onto mine with a ferocious hunger. His tongue explores every corner of my mouth, leaving me breathless and dizzy. Against the rough brick wall, he presses his body into mine, one hand sneaking up my dress to find my wet core.

"You're so fucking beautiful," he growls in my ear as he thrusts his fingers inside me.

• • •

I moan, my body arching into his touch. "People...could...see," I whisper.

"Let them see," he says fiercely. "I want them to know I am claiming you." With another hard thrust of his fingers, I come undone against his hand, pleasure mixing with fear in a heady rush.

"You taste so good," he says with a wicked grin, licking his fingers slowly and never taking his eyes off me. "Can't wait to fuck you."

"I want you," I plead.

"When I say so," he responds with a smirk. He walks towards an old yellow Mustang and hops in. "Are you coming?"

I follow him obediently, feeling like I'm in a trance. We drive through the streets of Vedado to Havana forest along the Malecón and finally arrive at Revolution Square. Alejandro's hand never leaves my thigh, always teasing and making my body ache for more. My mind can't focus on the sights - all I can think about is how he looks at me with such possessiveness and desire.

We drive along a narrow, winding road through the thick, humid forest of El Bosque de la Habana. Suddenly, he slams on the brakes and pulls into a secluded area hidden by overgrown vegetation.

Without warning, he growls, "I want you," and drags me into the backseat of the car. His rough voice sends shivers down my spine as his lips trail down to my neck, nipping at my skin. "You're mine," he whispers possessively.

He pulls my dress up and pushes aside my lacy white panties before plunging his face between my legs, tongue lapping at me. I cry out, my fingers tangling in his hair. It feels so good I can barely stand it.

"Ah, fuck, you taste so good," he moans into my pussy as he begins to eat me out, his cock rubbing against the entrance teasingly.

"I'm going to make you scream," he promises. My walls pulsing around his tongue, my need for him reaching a fever pitch.

I don't know how much more I can take, but I want it all. "Please, fuck me now."

He pulls back, looking up at me, his eyes burning with lust and otherworldly possession. He lifts me up, placing a pillow on the back seat and positioning himself between my legs. He slams into me, filling me so good and deep. His hands press against the car window, holding him up. He's big and thick, and every inch of him claims me possessively as he starts to move.

"You're so tight," he growls, each thrust a claim, "Mine," he groans as he pistons into me, his hips slapping against my ass. I can feel every powerful thrust deep inside. The sunlight streams through the trees, illuminating our bodies as he fucks me over and over.

"You feel so good," he growls into my ear.

My scream echoes in the forest as I cum hard around him. Alejandro follows soon after, groaning my name as he releases inside me. Tears sting at my eyes - such pleasure I've never felt before.

I feel completely exposed and yet full of life like never before. His touch marks me everywhere, both inside and out.

4

ALEJANDRO

The heat of Havana clings to our skin like a second layer as we roam the streets daily, the city's vibrant colors and pulsing life a backdrop to the intensity between us. Emma's laughter is a melody that dances with the rumba rhythms echoing from open doorways, and her inquisitive eyes sparkle with wonder at each historical treasure I unveil to her. She is a vision, feisty and free, blending into the tapestry of my homeland while standing out like the rarest gem.

"Tell me something about you that no one else knows," she whispers against my ear as we sway to the music in a dimly lit club. But I can't bring myself to do it. My past is buried deep within me, its weight too heavy to bear when every moment with her feels like soaring toward the sun.

"Mi amor, let's not talk now," I murmur back, the husky timbre of my voice betraying the desire that surges through me.

. . .

Under the cloak of darkness each night, I worship her body with an intensity that leaves both breathless, reducing my world to the space where our bodies meet. And as she cries out my name, I feel myself unraveling, walls crumbling as I give into this love that consumes me.

The ring of my phone slices through the humid air, a discordant note against the symphony of our breaths. I untangle myself from the warmth of Emma's limbs. With a heavy heart, I reach for the device, its glow an unwelcome intrusion in the cocoon of our intimacy.

"Abuela?" My voice is a raw whisper, every muscle tensed as I brace for the inevitable. "I understand. I'm coming."

Emma's gaze pierces through me, a storm of questions in her eyes. Her chest heaves with each breath, the sheets barely clinging to the curve of her hips.

"What's wrong? Talk to me," she implores, her voice a velvet whisper that somehow cuts through the chaos in my mind.

"Mi abuelita," I begin, the words tasting like ash in my mouth. "My grandmother is dying ... she needs me—I have to go."

. . .

Her mouth parts, a silent protest forming, but I cannot wait for her response. Time is a luxury I no longer possess. I press a fervent kiss to her forehead, a promise of return, and dress in haste, ignoring the clenching in my gut at the sight of her lying there, vulnerable and alone.

As I race through the streets of Havana, the night air slaps against my skin, and the city's vibrant pulse starkly contrasts the numbness spreading through my veins. My fingers tighten around the steering wheel, each turn taking me further from Emma, her scent still clinging to my skin like an invisible brand.

The weight of my family's legacy presses down on me as heavy as the humid air that fills my lungs. The car stops before the sprawling mansion that bears my true name, the weight etched into its stone facade.

At Abuela's bedside, her frail hand grips mine with surprising strength, her voice a fading whisper. "Todo para ti, Alejandro. You must decide now."

The weight of her words crushes me, not just the inheritance of wealth and power but the realm of an under-world I was trying to escape.

"Te amo, Tita," I murmur, my grip tightening on her hand.

"Todo para ti," she repeats with her dying breaths.

. . .

The decision is made; my course is set.

Abuela's words hammer against my skull as I descend the marble steps: "Everything to you. You are the head of the family now." Power, wealth, and control of Havana's underworld—all mine to wield. But I can't shake the image of Emma alone in my bed, the taste of her still lingering on my lips. She is my tempest, my fire—and I will return to claim her, come hell or high water. Because possession is not just taking; it's belonging. And Emma belongs to me, just as irrevocably as I belong to her.

5

EMMA

As the hours tick by, I make my way through the bustling streets of Havana, waiting for Alejandro's return. But he once vibrant atmosphere has shifted into a tense stillness, filled with hushed whispers floating on the air like ghostly echoes. Whispers that carry a heavy weight, pressing against my chest and tightening my throat.

"Carmelita Costa García is dead," they say in hushed tones, as if speaking her name aloud would summon her back to life.

Her death has left a void, and her grandson has stepped up to fill it. And as the name "El Jefe" reverberates around me, fear and reverence mingling in equal measure, it hits me like a ton of bricks.

"Abuelita..."

. . .

My heart seizes in terror as realization crashes over me like a tidal wave. El Jefe, the new leader of Havana's criminal world, is none other than Alejandro. My Alejandro. The man who ignited every fiber of my being with a single touch, whose possessive gaze can unravel me in seconds.

I stagger backwards, the street suddenly spinning out of control. How could it be the same man who whispered sweet promises into my skin at night, whose strong hands claimed every inch of me with an intensity I couldn't resist?

A nauseous surge of adrenaline courses through me. I need to escape—to leave behind the heat of his touch and the intoxicating scent of his cologne that still lingers on my skin. The very essence of him that has become my addiction is now laced with venom.

Every cell in my body screams for him, yearning for his commanding presence, yet I know I have to flee. I have to sever the ties that bind us to protect my heart from shattering beyond repair. How can I trust him?

The quaint cobblestone streets that once sang of romance now whisper warnings. The soft sea breeze that had tangled through my hair during our moonlit walks now pushes me towards salvation. I can't look back. Not even for the man who made me feel more alive than ever before. Not when his love is built on secrets and shadows.

6

ALEJANDRO

Sweat beads on my forehead as I rush through the crowd of people, each step amplified by the pounding in my chest. The streets of Havana are a blur, faces merging into an indistinct canvas of colors and expressions.

"Emma," I murmur, a mantra to keep me anchored. She doesn't know the truth, not all of it. The dark legacy I inherited was never meant to touch her world, but it has, and now she's slipping through my fingers like fine sand. I feel it in my bones.

The door slams behind me, echoing through the empty house like a gunshot. I'm breathing hard, sweat slick on my brow, my heart a violent thunder in my chest. Clothes are missing, the scent of her perfume a lingering ghost that claws at my insides.

• • •

"Damn it, Emma," I curse under my breath, my voice a low rumble of frustration and fear. Her suitcase is gone. I've pushed her to this edge, and now I'm teetering on the precipice of losing her.

"Emma!" My roar is futile; she's not here to hear it. Time is slipping through my fingers, grains of sand that mock with their inevitable descent. I sprint back out, desperation lending speed to my steps. I have to find her. I need to make this right.

I drive around hopelessly, scanning the sea of cars, searching for the one carrying away the woman who owns every inch of my possessive, desperate soul. And then I see a yellow taxi cutting through the haze.

She is there—I catch a glimpse of her face in the rearview mirror, a fleeting vision. The taxi slows, brakes squealing, a screech that sings of second chances.

I slam my break and stop right in front.

The driver looks at me, recognition dawning like a slow, inevitable sunrise. He reads the situation as if it's a script he's known all his life. With a silent nod that speaks volumes of Havana's unspoken codes, he vacates the taxi, abandoning the keys in the ignition and leaving us alone.

· · ·

"Emma," I start, my voice rough like gravel yet laced with an urgency that trembles through our shared space. My hands, large and commanding, capture hers, so delicate and quivering.

"I need you to hear this." Her breath hitches, eyes wide, irises swirling pools of confusion and hurt. I press on, knowing this is the only chance I have to bridge the chasm that's opened between us.

"Emma, mi amor," I whisper, my thumb caressing the soft skin of her hand. "I've lived a life cloaked in shadows. But you've seen through the darkness. You've touched a part of me that I thought was lost forever." My grip tightens, a silent plea for her to understand the depth of my confession. Her skin is warm and smooth against my calloused palms.

"Emma, mi vida," the words heavy with emotion. "From the moment I laid eyes on you, I knew you were meant to be mine. Every second apart from you is a painful ache that consumes me."

My confession spills out, my heart pouring out all the raw truths and desires I've held back for so long. "I can't promise you a life without struggles or one filled with honesty. Not now. But I will love you fiercely and protect you with every fiber of my being until the end of time... Will you marry me?"

• • •

Her eyes glisten, tears brimming on the edge of a precipice, and her lips part as if she was about to speak, but no words come out. My heart races a drumbeat, waiting, craving her answer.

"Please," I whisper, unable to hold back any longer, my lips grazing hers in a torment of nearness. "Say yes."

"Si," she whispers back, surrendering to the storm.

EPILOGUE
EMMA

The first rays of Valentine's Day filter into our room, casting a warm glow over entwined limbs and shared breaths. Alejandro's touch is seared into my skin, a sign of the night gone by.

"Happy anniversary, mi amor," his voice, deep and resonant, still sends shivers down my spine, even after all this time.

I turn to face my husband, whose mere presence commands respect on the bustling streets below us, where whispers of his power dance on the tongues of those who dared speak his name. But here, in the sanctity of our silk sheets, he is my Alejandro, my fierce protector.

"Five years," I breathe, my lips inches from his, "and you've kept every promise."

. . .

His eyes speak of an unquenchable fire and tender devotion —a duality only I am privileged to witness. And he is the only one who could ever peel back the layers of my soul, leaving me bare and wanting.

"Te amo," I whisper, my hands venturing up to tangle in his thick, dark hair, pulling him closer until there is no space between us.

"Y yo a ti," he replies, his lips capturing mine. My body responds to his every command, each touch a decree, each whisper a law unto itself.

I feel his hard cock lengthening, pushing in my entrance. He fills me up , staking his claim all over again, reminding me that I am his. My body responds to his every command, each touch a decree, each whisper a law unto itself. I call his name over and over, and I don't care who can hear us.

I searched all my life for this pleasure and abandonment— the raw edge of life, the dance of danger and desire, and I found it in the Havana heat in his arms.

BARCELONA DREAMS

1

MIA

The sun radiates a golden glow on the bustling market, and a chilly breeze nips at my cheeks. The merchants have just finished setting up their stalls, each proudly displaying their treasure for the day. I arrive early, eagerly anticipating my weekly visit to the Mercat Dominical del Llibre de Sant Antoni. As I walk through the rows of stalls, the musty scent of old books fills my senses, and I can't help but smile.

I make my way to my favorite stall filled with rows upon rows of leather-bound tomes and dusty texts. Each spine holds the promise of a new adventure, and I can't resist running my fingers along them as I search for hidden treasures. My heart flutters with excitement as I lose myself in books.

And then I see it - a small book tucked between two larger texts. It is unassuming, but something about it catches my eye. My hands quiver with excitement as I carefully slide it from its resting place, a cloud of dust swirling in the morning light. Its cover creaks as I open it, revealing yellowed pages filled with elegant script. A love letter!

My eyes dart over the words, devouring their poetic beauty. I can almost imagine the sender penning this intimate confession by candlelight. I can't believe my luck as I read each word, savoring the emotion that spill from every page. I love this place!

"Why does no one write love letters anymore?" I mutter, longing for a love of other times.

My eyes drift up from my book to the shadow that looms over me. A tall, dark-haired man stands before me, his chiseled jawline and piercing dark eyes leaving me breathless. My mind starts to wander ...

"Carlos," he says and extends a hand across the table. My heart races at the possibility of a meet-cute straight out of a romance novel.

"Mia," I reply.

But then his words shatter the illusion. "A dreamer, I see." he scoffs, his eyes lingering on the cover of my chosen book before meeting mine with a smirk. "Romance novels only ruin relationship in the real world." His tone is dripping with superiority and condescension.

. . .

I can feel my face flush with anger, my mind already forming arguments about the power of love and the magic found within the pages of these novels. Austen and Brontës... Instead, I take a deep breath and slide the letter back into place before snapping the book shut.

"To each their own," I say and brush past him, feeling the comforting weight of the colorful maze of books surrounding me once again.

"It's not true," I whisper to myself as I run my fingers over the spines of each book.

Somewhere out there, someone will sweep off my feet and write me verses sweeter than aged wine, showing his desire through the stroke of a pen. Until then, I'll continue my search for hidden magic in the pages of these books.

2

CARLOS

The sun beats down on the back of my neck as I follow her through the bustling market. Her hair cascades over her shoulders in soft, bouncy curls, and her bright eyes sparkle in the sunlight. My gaze can't help but linger on her tempting lips, pink and plump with a slight sheen of gloss. She wears a light coat that hugs her curves in all the right places, accentuating her ample breasts and round behind. I am completely mesmerized by her. I want to lose myself inside her folds and make her mine forever.

Suddenly, today is filled with promise...

As we weave through the stalls, she pauses at a bookstall and delicately runs her fingers over the rows of antique bindings. A look of excitement lights up her face as she discovers something tucked between the pages of a worn novel. My mind races, my cock is stirring.

· · ·

I have to talk to her. But before I realize I blurt something out that clearly upsets her. I've never been good at expressing my feelings. Never had to. People jump when I speak, ready to fulfill my every wish. Damn.

Mia. Even her name is music to my ears.

I can't let her walk out of my life. I observe her closely as she browses through the market stalls, trying to figure out what made her smile before I messed it up. And then I find it - a handwritten love letter.

"Why not?" I think. I am much better at writing than talking about my feelings. She is a romantic at heart.

I will leave her secret love letters, leading her on a scavenger hunt to discover my true feelings. Fourteen letters, fourteen days leading up to Valentine's Day. Until she is mine.

As Mia leaves the bustling market, I follow her through the winding streets of the Sants until she disappears into a grand building. I watch as she fumbles with her keys and unlocks the heavy door. A warm glow spills from one of the windows.

Later that night, I sit at my desk, pen in hand, and begin writing my confession on a parchment paper. The ink smudges slightly as I scrawl:

. . .

Querida,

your adventure starts now. I long to be the one who shows you all the passion and ecstasy your heart desires. Let me take you away from this world into misty folds and hidden depths that only we will discover together. My heart and body belong to you, Mia, to cherish or neglect as you please.

I will reveal myself to you soon. Look for your next clue at the Basilica de la Sagrada Familia, in the crypt."

I hide the note between the pages of Wuthering Heights, leaving a sticky note with her name on it. I can almost feel her delicate fingers brushing against it as she discovers my secret message.

I yearn to hear my name escape from her lips in surprise. My mind races with thoughts of feeling her melt under my touch. But for now, I must wait and savor the anticipation. I am consumed by the desire for her, longing to hold her in my arms and explore every inch of her body. The waiting will only intensify my burning desire for her.

. . .

But patience is key; I know she will be mine, no matter what it takes.

3

MIA

I approach my mailbox, and the familiar scent of metallic rust and paper clings to my nostrils. Standing out among the usual stack of mundane bills and advertisements is an old copy of Wuthering Heights with my name on it. I grasp it eagerly, feeling the slightly rough texture under my fingertips. Inside the book there is an ivory envelope; I open it carefully, unfolding the crisp paper, heart hammering, a wild thing in my chest.

"Querida," it begins; my heart races as I read the words, each one a sensual caress on my skin, "Your adventure starts now."

The words dance before me, ink swirling with promises and secrets. I inhale the scent of paper, imagining the writer, mysterious and unseen. My pulse quickens as I read on, devouring the lines, my mind painting vivid images of hidden paths and unknown destinations. A challenge laid bare.

• • •

"Find the next clue at the Basílica de la Sagrada Familia, in the crypt."

Every morning, I stand at the edge of my mundane existence, staring out from my tiny balcony as if waiting for a sign, wishing for more. More than routine, more than predictable days that bleed into each other without distinction. The universe has heard my silent pleas, finally.

"Follow the trail," it now whispers, "Let your heart guide you."

And so I do. Each day, I make my way through the cobblestone streets of Barcelona, following addresses and cryptic notes left for me by some unknown sender. But everywhere I go, there's Carlos; our paths seem to cross like magic every day. At the corner café, he's there, his gaze heavy on my back. He's there, in the shadowed nooks, watching, waiting. Always a step ahead or behind, like a dance we're both learning the steps.

"Lost again, Mia?" His voice, a low rumble, wraps around me, tender and warm.

"Never lost," I reply with a smile that doesn't quite reach my eyes. "Just... exploring."

• • •

His presence is a magnetic field that both alarms and thrills me. There's a tension between us that crackles with every shared glance or fleeting encounter. And each one leaves me breathless—his nearness unsettling.

"Be careful," he warns, eyes darkening with something fierce, something protective.

"Always am," I reply, the lie smooth on my tongue. I'm anything but careful, chasing moonlight, craving the unknown. With every meeting, the tension coils tighter.

Yet the letters consume me, every word pulling me deeper into a sea of longing. They promise passion and freedom, a chance to lose myself in unbridled love. Each letter is a caress from afar, a seduction by words that paint desire in hues I didn't know existed. I crave the total abandon they promise, the chance to loose—and find—myself.

Who is writing these letters? Who is this stranger who seems to know exactly what I crave?

I clutch the latest letter to my chest; the mystery is a flame; I am the moth, drawn irrevocably to its light. I want more— more clues, more letters, more of the man who sees me with smoldering eyes.

"Who are you?" I whisper again, this time into the warmth of a Barcelona night, the question hanging in the air.

. . .

With each step, I'm closer to the truth, closer to unraveling the desires woven into these burning messages. And I am utterly, hopelessly captivated with every beat of my rebellious heart.

4

MIA

I sink down into the bathtub, allowing the warm water to envelope my body; the floral scent of lavender and jasmine engulfs me, but I cannot calm the whirlwind of emotions inside. With trembling hands, I hold the last letter, a piece of his soul, before our first meeting tomorrow.

Already, I know he is mine, this man who poured his soul onto paper for me. Mine, even though we haven't met.

I unfold the page, eagerly devouring each word.

"Mia,

I long to taste you, feel your skin under my tongue and teeth, and mark you as mine. I crave the sound of your moans and your *pleas for more. I ache for the taste of your sweetness, the salty tang of your desire."*

Shit! My hands shake as my eyes dart back to the mirror, imagining his lips against mine, his fingers tracing every curve of my body. My breath comes in short gasps as my imagination runs wild. I'm sure he knows what he is doing to me.

I push my hand between my legs. This is what he wants, what he desires. My fingers tentatively explored my swollen folds, teasing at my clit, circling it gently before plunging inside. I moan at the feeling, the need growing stronger than ever.

I reread his words, "I will kiss every inch of you until you beg for me," I give into the ache and press two fingers deep inside myself. My hips roll, meeting his rhythm, my breath catching in my throat.

"Yes," I breathe, my body taking control as I thrust harder, faster. I am lost in his words, in the images they paint in my mind. He owns me, body and soul.

I let out a low, desperate whimper, imagining it was him, his voice in my ear. "Please."

· · ·

My thumb presses on my clit, circling it roughly, and I cum with a cry that fills the room. It was unlike anything I'd ever felt before - raw, primal, and freeing.

These letters have awakened a new hunger within me - one for dominance and power. For a man who commands what he desires, unafraid to claim it as his own. A man who would make me his in every sense.

My heart is pounding, and my body is humming. This is what I need. This is what I want.

5

CARLOS

I make my way through the bustling city streets; I can feel the weight of the secret I'm about to reveal press against my chest like a stone. The Fountain of Lights stands tall and proud in the center of the square, its water shimmering from the reflection of neon lights.

And then I see her - Mia, standing with her back to me, her red coat hugging her curves perfectly. Her hair cascades down her back like a flowing river of silk. The scent of her perfume drifts towards me on the gentle breeze. My chest tightens with nerves, and I take deep breaths to calm myself down. This is the moment I've been waiting for.

I clear my throat, and Mia turns to face me. Her eyes meet mine for an electric second before annoyance flashes across her face, quickly turning to confusion.

"Carlos?" She asks. "What are you doing here?"

. . .

"I wanted to see you," I say, my voice low and husky.

"Have you been following me?" She gaps.

"Every step," I confess, my voice raw with emotion. "Since the first day I saw you."

I can see the wheels turning in her head. I hold up the red rose, the sign.

Her eyes widen in disbelief. "No, ... you can't ... " she murmurs, unable to finish the sentence.

"Open the letter, "I command softly. Mia hesitates for a moment before pulling it out of her handbag, her breath coming faster now. Slowly, she unfolds the paper, and I begin reciting out loud: "I want to taste you, feel you, possess you..."

"To consume you and be consumed ... deeply..."

I take the letter from her fingers and continue the words I know so well, stepping closer: "I want to mark my claim on you, make you scream my name until there's no tomorrow."

. . .

Mia's lips part in shock, her eyes wide with wonder and desire. She starts to speak, but no words come out.

"I love you, Mia, I want you, I need you."

She trembles beneath my touch as I tilt her chin up, forcing her to look into my eyes. The desire in her gaze mirrors my own. Without warning, I crash my lips onto hers, taking her in a fierce and passionate kiss. She responds with equal fervor, her hands slipping into my hair, pulling me closer still. I taste her sweetness, feel her warmth against me, the softness of her curves.

My possessive nature takes over, and I nip at her bottom lip, demanding more from her. She moans into my mouth, surrendering entirely to my touch. We're both lost in a haze of lust and need, wanting more than just a simple kiss.

"Carlos.... I wanted it to be you," She melts into me, her body trembling with anticipation and want.

The Fountain of Lights comes alive with its powerful pumps spewing dancing jets of water accompanied by dazzling lights and a booming soundtrack as the sky turns dark.

"You are mine now!"

6

CARLOS

S he's warm and soft in my arms, her body moving against mine, her lips are eager, her mouth hungry. I can't get enough of her.

"Your place," I breathe out, and she nods, a hard jerk of her chin. We rush past Placa Espanya. I mold her body against mine as we weave through the winding streets of Sants, our footsteps echoing off the narrow walls of the old buildings.

My hand trails down her spine, stopping at the curve of her ass, and I give it a squeeze. She moans into my mouth, and I know we're both lost. There's no going back now. I'll claim her here, on these dusty cobblestones, if I have to. I pull her closer, grinding into her, feeling my hardness between her legs as she gasps. Her nails claw at my back, leaving little pinpricks that only serve to fuel the fire inside me.

• • •

We break apart for air, panting, and she looks up at me with hooded eyes. I want to make her mine. Mia is mine.

Finally, we reach her apartment building, and I grab her hand, leading her up the stairs two at a time. She's laughing, breathless, her breasts bouncing with every step. I can't help but catch a glimpse of them from the open coat, and my mouth waters. I need to taste them, to feel them against my lips. I push her against the wall, my lips finding hers again, my tongue tracing her mouth hungrily.

The door flings open, and we stumble inside. Her body melts into mine as I lift her up, carrying her inside. I slam the door shut behind us, the sound of the lock clicking into place, sending a jolt of possessiveness through my veins. She's mine.

Her living room is dimly lit, the only light coming from a small lamp on the coffee table. I push her against the wall, pinning her with my body, and kiss her again, harder this time. Our teeth clash, and I want to mark her like an animal. To brand her as mine. She gasps, and it only spurs me on.

Fumbling with her coat, I finally have it off her shoulders, baring her perfect body to my greedy touch. I trail my fingers down her stomach, dipping into the valley between her breasts. She arches into me, and I groan, the sound vibrating against her lips. My other hand finds the zipper of her dress, and soon, she's stepping out of it, standing before me in just her bra, lace thong, and heels. Fuck. My hands cup her ass, squeezing the full cheeks as I devour her lips, my other hand moving up to grope her core.

She's soaking wet, already begging for me. I breathe hard against her neck, whispering dirty promises in her ear. I spin her around and whip off my shirt, panting heavily, "Bedroom," I growl, her moans fueling my desire.

"First on the left," she moans in my ear.

The mattress springs creak under our weight as I push her down, my lips never leaving hers. I fumble with the clasp of her bra. My teeth graze her skin as I pull it off, dropping it to the floor. Her breasts spill into my palms, warm and inviting. I take one in my mouth, sucking on her nipple as I kneel down.

"Carlos," she moans as she arches her back, her fingers raking through my hair.

I stand back up, my hands traveling down her body, skimming over her stomach and hips to the waistband of her thong. With a swift tug, it's gone.

"You are so fucking beautiful," I gasp at the sight of her, her curves and contours on full display. Her scent fills my senses - she bites her bottom lip, watching me hungrily. I whip off my shirt, panting heavily. My cock throbs, aching against my jeans. "On your knees," I growl.

. . .

She does as she's told, gazing up at me. I push her hair from her face, my hand running through it. I breathe heavily as I unbutton my jeans and push them down, freeing my aching shaft. "Take me in your mouth," I pant, my hand gripping the back of her head.

She takes me deep, her lips touching the very base of my dick before wrapping them around me, and I groan harshly.

"That's it," I growl. She is sucking and licking me as if she's starved for it. Her lips and tongue work in tandem, milking me. My hips jerk forward, driving deeper into her mouth. Her eyes are closed, and a small whimper escapes her lips.

She's mine. Only mine.

"Oh Fuck." The word is torn from my throat. "That's it, baby." Her hair is a wild mane around her face as she bobs up and down on me, taking as much of my length as she can handle. I grab her hair, pulling her up gently, "On the bed," I command, and she obeys without question.

I crawl over her slowly, pinning her wrists above her head with one hand as I thrust into her soft warmth. Her legs wrap around my waist, pulling me closer still. She's so tight I can barely contain the groan bubbling up in my throat. She is worth every second of the wait.

. . .

I bite her shoulder playfully, nibbling on the taught skin before kissing it softly. She tastes like freedom and passion - just like Barcelona herself. My other hand gropes her breast roughly, pinching the nipple between my fingers until she gasps for breath.

"Caaaarlos," she moans out, arching into me even more. Damn, I do love the sound of my name on her lips.

"You belong to me," I growl against her neck, thrusting harder into her wet heat. She's mine now; no one else's.

She cries, "Yes," her voice rough and needy, "you own me."

I pick up the pace, slamming into her with urgency. Her body meets mine stroke for stroke, her loud moans filling the room. Her nails dig into my back as she grinds down on me. "Fuck," I pant, pulling my hips back from her throbbing core, only to slam back inside her. "You feel so damn good," I groan, my mouth finding hers once more.

"Yes," she hisses between breaths, eyes closed in bliss and desire. I reach down, finding her clit with one rough finger and circling it, watching as she buckles underneath me. She cries out my name, so close to release, right to the edge. I slap her ass hard before plunging inside of her one last time, feeling her walls clench around me.

. . .

I pull out, and she begs, purring like a kitten.

"I'm not done with you, "I say, "remember? I want to mark my claim on you, make you scream my name until there's no tomorrow?"

I turn her around and spread her ass cheeks; I press my cock against her tight asshole, and she whimpers, "I have never done... aaa..." and she screams as I plunge in her ass, pounding her, filling her up. She takes it all. My fingers find her clit once more, and I rub it with a rough grip until she cums hard on my fingers.

Fuck," I grit out, feeling my own orgasm build inside me. I hold her tight against me and fill her again with one last hard thrust before emptying myself inside of her, shuddering and growling against her neck.

"Mine," I groan into her skin, holding onto this moment of freedom amidst the chaos of Barcelona.

EPILOGUE

MIA

The scent of roses envelopes me, the color of passion sprawled across our kitchen table—a crimson sea dotted with envelopes. White, pristine, each one a vessel of ardor and ink. Carlos has sent them every month for three years like clockwork, his words melting into paper, a fervent cascade from his heart to mine.

I trace a fingertip over today's envelope, the edges sharp, the surface smooth—unmarred by time or doubt.

Three years. The soft scratch of pen on parchment echoes in my mind, Carlos' confessions unfurling in loops and swirls of script.

Cracking the seal, I unfold today's letter. His handwriting dances before my eyes— each sentence pulls me deeper and tethers me tighter.

· · ·

"Mi amor," it begins, the endearment a caress against my skin. Ink bleeds devotion, painted scenes of us lost in places where horizons stretch endlessly. Carlos' letters are maps of desire charted in his steady hand.

I press the paper to my lips, the texture whisper-soft, imagining his touch, firm yet tender—a paradox that defines the man I love. His possession is a flame, consuming and illuminating the darkest parts of my being.

My lips part, whispering his name, an invocation, a surrender. It's desire, raw and unapologetic. I close my eyes and see his face; my heart—is no longer mine. It beats for him, a rhythm composed by his hand, his will.

His love letters are not just paper and ink. They are whispers, promises, and commands that resonate through my core. Each one a step closer to the edge, where control teeters and falls away, leaving me bare, open, his.

I am his compass, his north star, navigating through storms and still waters. And he, my captain, my conqueror, charting a course that leads always, inevitably, back to his arms.

Carlos, my love, my everything. In your possession, I am free.

MARRAKESH MAGIC

E

1

JEAN-CLAUDE

A new day begins in Marrakech, the amber sun filtering through my window. I stretch, feeling the ache of yesterday's labor fade away. My body is a honed instrument.

Splashing cool water on my face, I dress simply and head outside to the bustling medina. A symphony of noise greets me - vendors shouting, spices perfuming the air, and the chatter of early risers.

I navigate through the twisting alleys with ease, standing out as an oddity among the locals. But they accept me, knowing I have proven myself.

I order my regular café noir at my local cafe and sip it slowly as I take the morning rush around me. The city comes to life - children playing, mothers bartering, donkey carts clattering alongside mopeds. But I am grounded in this place - the scents of spices, flowers, and smoke filling my lungs. Marrakech is my refuge, where the past stays buried, and each new day promises a fresh start.

And now it's time for work - shaping metal, hefting stone, tending to the earth. But for now, I allow myself a moment of stillness before diving into another day full of promise and possibilities.

I gulp the last of my coffee and toss a few dirhams on the counter. The day beckons, and I have work to do. A stone wall awaits me, eager for my rough-hewn hands to shape it into place.

Building, not destroying. Creating, not tearing down. This work soothes the festering wounds in my soul.

As I walk through the city, people greet me with familiarity and warmth. I am no longer an outsider here. My trust has been earned through hard work and sweat. Turning a corner, I see the wall that needs my attention - a small home desperately needing repair. I set down my tools and flex my calloused fingers in anticipation. There is solace in honest work beneath this scorching desert sun.

With each rock I lift and place, the wall takes shape under my skilled hands. The roughness of the stones scrapes against my palms, but it's a familiar pain that comforts me. Out of the corner of my eye, I see Amina emerging from her home, her veil fluttering lightly in the breeze. Our eyes meet, and she nods in gratitude. Her simple acknowledgment is all the payment I need.

Focusing on the task at hand, I lose myself in the rhythm of the work. The repetitive motions still my restless mind. No thoughts of the past or worries about the future. Just this moment, this wall, this stone to be laid.

Sweat drips down my face as I work, slamming rocks into place with my hammer. The midday sun beats down on me, but I don't care. It's cleansing, just like the work I'm doing.

Chiseling away at rough edges, I fit each rock carefully into the growing wall. One by one, they take shape until the final stone slots perfectly into place. The sun is setting when I finish. This wall is a symbol of potential and redemption for even the most damaged stones - maybe even for me.

Wiping my brow, I pack my tools and head through the bustling medina. Vendors call out their wares, and children play, but I stay focused on my path. Suddenly, an elderly woman catches my eye. She's struggling under the weight of her bags, her face wrinkled with effort. I offer to help without hesitation.

She startles at first but then gratefully hands over her bags. With ease, I load them onto her cart.

"Alhamdulillah," she says with a smile.

. . .

A faint warmth rises inside me. "yarhamuk Allah," I reply.

The sun sets as I rush through winding alleys, the world cooling around me. Children's laughter echoes in my mind, a moment of fleeting joy. An old man carves wood outside his shop, wise eyes nodding at my passing. The aroma of fresh bread pulls me towards a bakery, but I resist. There are debts to pay before I can rest.

Merchants pack up as the city gates loom closer. The last customers haggle loudly before disappearing into the night. Soon, the streets are empty except for the occasional passerby. I embrace the solitude and shadows, hiding from my past sins until dawn breaks once more.

My footsteps echo off the stone walls as I walk through the streets. Memories of my troubled past creep in, threatening to consume me. I quicken, desperate to outrun the demons lurking in the darkness. But they follow me relentlessly, their whispers growing louder with each shadow. Flashes of violence, of lives destroyed by my hands. I clench my fists and steady myself for the long night ahead. The alleys narrow, and shadows creep along the cracked walls.

Monsters come out to play at this hour.

. . .

I pause at a huddled figure - a child shivering against the chill. I offer him bread from my satchel and move on. My riad appears, but I remain wary.

Sanctuary rarely lasts long in these streets.

The heavy door creaks open, and I am enveloped in stillness. A candle flickers to life and I sink into my familiar armchair, the leather warm and comforting. A gentle breeze carries the scent of jasmine through the open window. Eyes closed, I listen to crickets chirping in a hypnotic melody.

The city noise fades away, leaving only peace. Shadows dance with the flickering candlelight.

My thoughts drift back to the people I encountered today. In them, I found pockets of hope amidst the hardship. Moments of human connection to cherish. For them, I continue my solitary fight against the evil lurking in this ancient city. Because no one else can or will.

For now, I close my eyes once more and breathe. Breathe.

2

JEAN-CLAUDE

The alleyways of the medina pulse with life. Vendors hawk their wares, crowds jostle, and chatter. Incense and spices perfume the air. This is the Marrakech I know, yet today, it feels different. Electric.

The cause soon becomes clear - her. That woman there, with the windswept hair and searching eyes. An American tourist. But different from the others, content to cling to their guidebooks and pre-planned itineraries. No, I sense her spirit runs free like the alley cats that prowl these streets.

She pauses at a pile of handwoven rugs, fingering the tassels, eyes bright with curiosity. My pulse quickens at the sight. How long since someone ignited such fire in my blood? I abandoned passion long ago, along with my old life. Now, my days run smooth and uncomplicated. But watching her, I ache. To harness that wildness. Possess it fully.

.   .   .

Our eyes meet and lock. In that instant, I am lost, tossed back into the roiling seas of desire I thought I calmed forever. I should turn away, forget this encounter. Instead, I am drawn in.

"Can I help you with something?" she asks boldly.

"You can't resist me, can you?" I respond with a smirk.

"Dream on," she counters, raising an eyebrow at my arrogance.

"It's a fact." I say confidently, " I'm Jean-Claude. And you are ...?"

"None of your business," she replies, not backing down. I lean in closer, our faces only inches apart. "I always get what I want."

"Not this time," she retorts, pushing me away with unexpected strength. I grin, impressed by her fire and grit. This alley cat will take some taming. But as she disappears into the crowd, the scent of her perfume lingering, I know I will. Though she may wound me, the agony will be exquisite. I have found my match here on the streets of Marrakech.

.   .   .

I weave through the crowded market, trailing at a distance as she explores the stalls. She moves with carefree grace, fingering fabrics and haggling for trinkets, seemingly oblivious to the dangers behind these ancient walls.

Foolish girl. Does she not realize her golden hair and pale skin mark her as an outsider? In the shadows, eyes watch, waiting for a moment of inattention. While her spirit enchants me, I curse her recklessness. She must learn caution. And restraint.

When she wanders down an empty side street, I quicken my pace. As I'd feared, three men detach from the shadows. My heart pounds. I should call out, warn her away. But that would only startle them into action. So I melt into the darkness and circle behind them, ready. I am always ready.

She tries to push past, but they close ranks, leering. One grabs her wrist. She stomps his instep, then slaps his face fiercely. They stagger back, curses rising to their lips. My cue. I emerge from the shadows and pull her into the shelter of a doorway.

"This is no place for you," I murmur. Her eyes flash. She tries to jerk away. I tighten my grip while watching the men who have regained their footing.

"Trust me, you do." My voice is steel. She stills, reading the truth in my eyes. I look at them, and they know better than to fight me. I pull her into a narrow alley, pressing her against the cool clay wall. She struggles in my grasp, eyes blazing.

"Unhand me!" she hisses. "I don't need a bodyguard."

I lean in close, inhaling her jasmine scent. "You may not need one, but you have one regardless."

She tosses her head defiantly. "I can take care of myself."

"Can you?" My voice drops to a sensual murmur as I run my fingers along her arm. "*Tu as du courage*; I'll grant you that. But these streets hide dangers you cannot imagine."

Her breath catches at my touch even as annoyance flickers in her gaze. "You know nothing about me."

"I know you are impétueuse, " her eyes squint, "Reckless. Foolhardy," I explain. My lips graze her ear. "You require a firm hand." A tremor runs through her, though she tries to hide it. I meet her eyes. "I think you yearn for more than you know." My voice resonates with truth.

For a moment, she is silent, searching my face. Then she looks away. "I...I should go." But she makes no move to leave the circle of my arms. The air between us sizzles. I lean closer, and her lips part slightly as I draw near, her breath coming faster. Our bodies are a hairsbreadth away from touching, the space between us electric.

I brush my fingers along her jawline, and she shivers, eyes drifting closed. Slowly, hesitantly, her body bridges the distance between us igniting something primal within me. For a long moment, we stare at each other on the precipice of something dangerous and new.

I press my forehead to hers, struggling to rein in my raging need. "You should go," I say hoarsely.

"I should go," she whispers again but makes no move to leave. With a low growl, I crush her against me, claiming her mouth passionately. I pin her harder to the wall, reveling in her softness, inhaling her intoxicating scent. She clings to me, nails digging into my shoulders, a small moan escaping her lips. I trail kisses down her neck, nipping at the tender flesh. Her head falls back, back arching, silently begging for more.

A growl rumbles in my chest, and I crush my mouth to hers once more. She returns the kiss hungrily, nails raking down my back. I lift her effortlessly in one smooth motion, and her legs wrap around my waist. I know I should release her, but I cannot bring myself to let her go.

Not yet. Not ever.

.   .   .

I groan against her lips. "You are playing with fire." I want all of her, here and now.

Distantly, I hear voices approaching. With a snarl of frustration, I wrench myself away, breathing hard. She sags against the wall, cheeks flushed, lips swollen from my kisses. I step back, raking a hand through my hair. "This isn't over," I rasp.

Her eyes flash defiantly.

The voices near. With a final look, I melt into the shadows. The dance continues, but I know one thing: she will be mine.

3

SARAH

The bustling marketplace of Jemaa el-Fnaa bombards my senses, overwhelming me with a kaleidoscope of colors and scents. The vibrant textiles of crimson and gold swirl in front of my eyes while the tangy aroma of spices and sizzling street food fills my nostrils. The shrill notes of snake charmers' flutes pierce my ears, adding to the chaotic symphony around me.

That's when I see him again. Jean-Claude. Day after day, he has been there, watching over me.

His muscular frame towers over the locals, sunlight glinting off his chiseled features. Our eyes lock, and the din of the market fades into oblivion. It's just him, just us. Memories flood back to me - his lips on mine, his fingers tangled in my hair, his hard body pressed against mine. I crave more, need more.

· · ·

I know so little about him. His eyes - they hint at shadows and his moves at practiced fights. He stirs something deep within me, awakening a burning desire I've kept hidden for so long. I know there is danger lurking beneath his surface, but perhaps that very danger draws me closer.

My feet move of their own volition, carrying me towards him through the melee, pushing against the human tide. He doesn't move, letting me come to him. The space between us buzz-zz-zz-es.

We do not speak. We do not touch. We only stare, suspended in this moment, so much left unsaid.

The market is receding into white noise. Jean-Claude's eyes blaze with lustful intent, his gaze fixed on me. I raise my chin in challenge. I know we're poised on the edge of something that will irrevocably change me. I'm ready to leap.

But it is Jean-Claude who breaks the spell, his smooth French accent drawing me in. "You haven't told me your name," he murmurs.

"Sarah," I reply, my voice barely above a whisper.

"Sarr-ah," he repeats, his lips caressing each syllable. "Let me show you Marrakech." The way he says Marrakesh makes shivers run down my spine.

• • •

With a smile, he extends his hand towards me. I hesitate for only a moment before slipping my palm into his, feeling the warmth and strength of his grip. As we go through winding alleys, bustling crowds fade away, and busy stalls give way to tranquil courtyards bursting with jasmine and bird song. The aroma of exotic spices permeates the air, and wind chimes gently sing in the breeze.

Jean-Claude's hand lingers on my lower back as we pass by fragrant bakeries and Qur'anic schools, getting lost in the magic of Marrakesh. With him by my side, I feel safe, even if it pains me to admit it. His touch ignites a fire within me that I can't ignore.

As we turn a corner, I glimpse a hidden courtyard adorned with bursts of bougainvillea and draped with colorful archways. Jean-Claude leans in close, his breath hot against my ear. "Do you like what you see?" he whispers.

I meet his intense gaze and answer. "I want to see more," I hope he knows what I mean.

Without another word, he leads us down an even narrower alley until we emerge into a deserted place. I catch a hint of sandalwood scent in the breeze. He backs me against the wall, his body a solid wall of heat. I welcome his weight, heat, and passion building since we first locked eyes across the market.

• • •

"Sarah..." he murmurs. Before I can breathe, his lips capture mine in a kiss that obliterates all thoughts. I lose myself in his touch, my hands tangling in his hair as he pulls me closer, his hands possessive on my hips.

We break apart, both trembling, but the lingering taste of him remains on my tongue. His hand shakes slightly as it caresses my cheek.

"What are you doing to me?" I whisper, my voice betraying the fear and desire swirling inside me.

A dangerous smile tugs at the corners of his mouth. "Only what you want, ma chérie," he says in a low, seductive tone.

I glimpse a tattoo on his forearm, faded but unmistakable. A grenade with seven flames. Recognition stirs. My voice shakes. "That tattoo...you were a soldier?"

His jaw tightens, and he pulls away from me, cloaked in shadow. "The past is gone. Only the present matters now." His words hold a warning, and, for now, I let it go.

Day after day, he watches over me. And day after day we play our dance.

4

————

JEAN-CLAUDE

I watch the steady rise and fall of Sarah's chest as she stands in front of me. Her features are soft, lips slightly parted as her breath comes in quiet puffs.

A pang of longing shoots through me, and I reach out to brush a strand of hair from her face. She doesn't stir, untroubled. Not like me. Since we started this...whatever this is between us, my mind has been in turmoil. I've never felt about anyone the way I feel about Sarah. She sets my blood on fire and makes my heart race. When we're together, it's explosive, passionate, all-consuming. I want to drown myself in her. Lose myself completely.

But then come the doubts. The fear. I don't know how to do this. I don't know how to love someone with this kind of reckless abandon. What if she realizes I'm not enough? That this brooding, broken man can never give her what she needs? I know she feels the darkness inside me, senses the demons that haunt my past. One day, she'll tire. She'll leave.

· · ·

Panic rises in my chest, sharp and sudden. My breaths come faster. I can't lose her. I won't survive it. Not this time. I fight the urge to pull her close and never let go. I want to promise to be what she needs. But the words stick in my throat.

"Jean-Claude?" Her voice, laced with concern, startles me. I meet her eyes and see the questions there. Gently, she touches my cheek.

"It's nothing," I say quickly. "Just thinking."

She studies me for a long moment before shifting closer. "Talk to me."

The gentle command in her voice makes me ache. I want to unburden myself, bare my soul to her as I've never done with anyone. But the fear is clawing at me. What if she can't love the man beneath the mask?

So, instead, I kiss her. I pour everything I cannot say into it - the longing, the desire, the sheer terror of losing this fragile thing between us. This push and pull is exhausting.

Sarah pulls back from the kiss, her eyes searching mine. "Jean-Claude, you can't keep avoiding talking to me." Words stick in my throat.

. . .

When I don't respond, she cups my face in her hands. "Talk to me. Please," she is quiet for a moment then continues, "I'm falling for you, Jean-Claude."

Her words make my heart ache with hope. But just as I'm about to respond, my phone buzzes with an incoming text. I glance at the screen and freeze.

It's from an unknown number, just three words that make my blood run cold:

I'm back.

Sarah sees the look on my face and frowns. "What is it? What's wrong?"

I quickly pocket my phone, forcing my expression to remain neutral. "It's nothing. Just stuff."

She doesn't look convinced but lets it go. "We're not done talking about this."

I nod, my mind racing. I know exactly who sent that text. Benoit Dubois, the mercenary I busted during Operation Serval in Northern Mali. The man who swore he'd get revenge no matter what it took. Sarah is in danger. Just the thought makes my heart seize. I have to protect her, whatever it takes.

"I'll take you back to your hotel," I say abruptly.

"Now?" Sarah asks in surprise. "It's late..."

"I know. It won't take long." I kiss her and start moving. After I drop her off, I dial an old contact from my old days. "Pierre? JC. I need weapons. Untraceable. And I need them tonight."

My mind is made up. I failed to protect someone I loved once before. I won't make that mistake again. No matter what demons from my past I have to face, I will keep Sarah safe.

I pull up to a deserted warehouse on the edge of town. Pierre is already waiting, a duffel bag in hand. He doesn't ask questions as he passes it over. We both know what's at stake here.

"Merci," I say tersely, tossing him an envelope of cash. I wasted no time emptying my accounts after getting that text.

. . .

Back home, I stash the bag under the floorboards in my closet. I spend the night cleaning and loading my new acquisitions by the light of a single lamp. The familiar rituals are almost meditative, calming my racing mind. This is what I know - what I'm good at.

At my core, I'm still the ruthless operative trained to do whatever it takes to eliminate a threat. And that's precisely what I'll do to keep Sarah safe. She'll never have to know the dark lengths I'm willing to go for her. Some demons are better left buried.

I stash the last weapons and scrub my hands, removing any trace of gunpowder. I am ready.

5

JEAN-CLAUDE

I navigate the maze of winding cobblestone streets in Marrakech; my nose is filled with the rich aroma of spices and incense. My heightened senses take in every noise and sight around me.

I finally reach The Central House Marrakech Medina, where Sarah is staying. Despite the 24/7 security, Sarah is not safe. Dubois can easily slip past them unnoticed, as I have. With a deep breath, I step into the hotel's cool courtyard, my boots clicking against the smooth stone tiles. After a few moments of searching, I find her suite- number 29.

I don't want to scare Sarah, so I'll watch over her like from the shadows while I wait. The faint light from a single bedside lamp casts long shadows across the room, revealing Sarah's sleeping figure. She lies on the four-poster bed, one leg stretched out under the soft cotton sheets. Her breathing is steady and deep.

• • •

Her blonde hair is fanned out around her head like a golden halo, her lips parted ever so slightly. My eyes devour her curves, the rise and fall of her breasts against the fabric of her tank top.

I can see the doorknob moving. Dubois is here. My heart races as I clench my fists and slowly open the window, careful not to make a sound. Suddenly, he bursts into the room, and I lunge at him, our bodies tumbling and thrashing on the floor like wild animals in a savage brawl. Sarah's eyes fly open from the noise, and she watches in terror as we fight.

Suddenly, the room goes silent. Dubois lays motionless on the grounds. It is done.

A knock at the door interrupts, "Mademoiselle, is everything okay there?" security calls out.

I gesture to Sarah to send them away, and she does, but horror is etched on her face. She looks so vulnerable. I kneel beside her, cradling her in my arms. Her heart is pounding against my chest, her breath ragged and uneven. She feels small and fragile.

"Shh, ma chérie," I whisper against her ear, holding her trembling body. "I've got you... I got you." Her sweat and fear mingle together with the faint scent of something else... something sweet and enticing. I breathe deeply, trying to calm myself. "I won't let anyone hurt you, baby," I promise.

· · ·

I text Yusuf, my ex-army friend,

"I need a pickup and clean."

Sarah is shivering in my arms. In 30 minutes, Yusuf appears at the window. His eyes narrow at seeing Dubois's lifeless body on the floor. "You okay, brother?" he asks in a low voice. I nod. We can leave now.

"Come on, baby, we need to go." We drive into my riad. I motion her in, but she is still shaking. I press my body against hers, and I feel the heat radiating from her skin. My desire for her consumes me, drowning out any rational thoughts. I brush my lips against her ear, my voice hoarse with emotion.

"I never wanted to involve you in my past," I confess. "I was fighting for what's right, but I did things I'm not proud of." My throat tightens. "Things that haunt me."

My words are met with tears streaming down her cheeks. "But I don't want to be that man anymore," I plead. "I love you."

Her eyes widen as she pulls back to look at me. "What?" I cup her face and wipe away her tears with my thumbs. "I love you," I repeat, unable to contain the truth any longer. "I've loved you since the first moment I met you."

. . .

A groan escapes my lips as I claim her in a slow and deep kiss, pouring all of my emotions into it.

"I...I love you too," she finally utters between kisses, and it's like music to my ears. My hands roam over every inch of her body. This is it. This is what I've been waiting for.

"I want you so much," she gasps as I sweep into my arms and carry her to the bed. I tear off her clothes, desperate for her skin. Moans escape her throat as I revel in the feel of her naked body beneath my hands. She is mine - finally, mine to touch, mine to possess.

My mouth travels down her neck to her pulse point, and I bite, marking her as my own. She arches into the bite, her nails raking down my back. My kisses grow more frenzied, more needy.

"Mine," I whisper against her skin. She cries in response, her body trembling with anticipation. I push her thighs apart, my rough hands exploring every inch of her softness. I groan at the wetness between her legs, my cock throbbing against my pants. "You're so ready for me," I growl.

She nods frantically, her breath coming out in short gasps.

I pull away, slip off my clothes, and join her on the bed. I want to last all night, but I don't think I can. At least not the first time. I slide inside her in one hard thrust, filling her completely. She gasps as she adjusts to my size, the bed creaking under our weight.

My body pins hers to the mattress, my hips grinding against hers. Fast, hard. She meets each thrust with her own, our skin slapping together. The room echoes with our moans, the scent of sex and sweat thick in the air.

Her nails are digging deep into my back, leaving delicate trails of pain that I welcome. "Tell me what you like," I demand.

"Harder," she whimpers. God, this woman is killing me. I oblige, taking her with force as she begs for more. I can feel her walls clenching around me, my cock sliding in and out of her wet heat, her moans crescendoing into screams.

"Yes," she cries out, her body arching off the bed, meeting my thrusts. She's close. I thrust faster and harder, feeling her orgasm approach. I kiss her neck again and again as I push deeper, harder.

She cries out louder this time, milking me "Yes, YEEEES, Jean-Claaaaude," fuck, the sound of my name on her lips fuels me even more, driving me to take her harder - deeper.

"Come for me," I demand. And she does, her body shaking violently as she climaxes against me. Her screams echo in the air.

• • •

"You're so fucking beautiful," I groan my own release only seconds away. I explode inside of her.

We lie there entwined for hours, outside the city sleeps. Sarah in my arms, and the Marrakech magic is what life is all about. And I am never letting go. Ever.

EPILOGUE

SARAH

The air hums with the heady scent of jasmine and spices, the soul of Marrakesh pulsating under my skin. I stand on our rooftop terrace, a mosaic of color beneath the setting sun; the Atlas Mountains are cradling the horizon.

There is a certain magic here, woven through the tapestry of the bustling medina and quiet courtyards, an ancient whisper that speaks of passion and rebellion.

Jean-Claude's hands encircle my waist from behind, his presence a fortress around me. The world falls away until there is nothing but the rhythm of our breaths and the warmth of his body seeping into mine. He is the storm, calm, shadow, and flame, and I am willingly caught in his gravity.

. . .

"Ma chérie," he whispers, his voice a velvet caress against my ear, his lips finding the sensitive spot on my neck that never fails to make me melt.

"My love," he murmurs, a deep rumble that resonates through me. I lean back into him, the Moroccan sun's heat paling compared to his fire. We stand in silence for a moment, taking in the view of the bustling medina below us, the calls of vendors mingling with the evening chorus of the muezzins. This vibrant, chaotic, magical city that is our home. Jean-Claude turns me in his arms, one hand caressing my cheek, and I close my eyes, nuzzling against his palm.

"You are so beautiful," he says.

I open my eyes to find him staring at me with that familiar possessive hunger like I am the most precious thing in the world to him. His strong hands roam my body as I melt against him. We have forever to explore each other. I am his, just as he is mine. Magic.

VIENNA WALTZ

1

JOHN

The warm, golden light of the setting sun streams through the floor-to-ceiling windows of my study, bathing everything in a warm glow. I stand by the grand piano, fingers gliding over the ivory keys as a Chopin nocturne flows from my memory. The melancholy melody echoes in the room as I gaze out at Vienna's spires and rooftops stretching before me.

Memories flood my mind - memories of happier times when Emily's mother was still with us. Five years have passed since her death, but the pain still lingers like a dull ache in my chest. Once filled with laughter and warmth, this room feels empty and hollow without her.

My gaze drifts to the velvet sofa where Emily always sits, swinging her feet and humming to my playing. She is my one solace after losing her mother - the one thing that has kept me from drowning in darkness.

. . .

I sigh and move away from the piano, making my way to the bar. The crystal decanter glints in the dimming light, tempting me with the promise of oblivion. I yearn to lose myself in the burn of aged scotch, if only for a little while.

Just then, laughter and pounding footsteps echo from the corridor. "Papa! Papa!" I see Emily running into the room, clutching a violin case and beaming up at me with pure joy. "Danke, Papa! My very own violin, just like the girl on the TV! Now we can play music together."

My breath catches at her words. I can't help but smile and feel grateful for this little ray of light in my life. "Well then, let's hear you play, meine Kleine." Joy wells inside me, more potent than any scotch.

Emily giggles and opens the case with a flourish. A child-sized violin is nestled inside the crimson velvet, polished to a sheen. She lifts it out reverently and places it beneath her chin as I have shown her, drawing the bow across the strings. A wavering, quavering, but tuneful note rings out. Needs some work.

She beams, bouncing on her toes. "Do you think I can be as good as the musicians on TV someday, Papa?"

"You can achieve anything you set your mind to." I remind her, ruffling her hair, my mood lightening for the first time longer than I can remember. "What would you say to starting violin lessons with a proper teacher?"

. . .

"A real violin teacher? For me?" Emily gasps, clutching her violin tight. "Oh, Papa, could we? I would practice every single day, I promise!"

Chuckling, I nod. "I'll have my assistant start searching for the best violin instructor in Vienna tomorrow."I wipe a tear from the corner of my eye, my heart full to bursting.

Emily shrieks delightfully and throws her arms around my waist, squeezing me tight. "Thank you, Papa! This is the best day ever!"

I hug her close; my darling girl deserves the world; if I have anything to say about it, she will have every opportunity life can offer.

I meet with my assistant, Hans, the following day. "Did you have any luck finding violin instructors for Emily?"

Hans nods. "Ja, seine Exzellenz. After reviewing credentials and speaking with references, I have narrowed the candidates down to three highly qualified instructors." He hands me a tablet with a curated folder of profiles on each.

"The first is Frau Weber, an instructor at the University of Music and Performing Arts with over twenty years of experience teaching children. The second is Herr Muller, a violinist in the Vienna Philharmonic who gives private lessons. And the third is Fräulein Wolff, a young instructor who recently won an international music competition and has glowing reviews from students and parents alike for her patience and results."

My finger hovers over the screen, scrolling through the profiles of potential music teachers for my daughter. I pause on the last one, Fräulein Anna Wolff. Her blonde hair falls in sleek waves around her face, and her bright green eyes radiate kindness and warmth behind a pair of wire-rimmed glasses. Impressive credentials from a prestigious music conservatory and glowing student reviews make her stand out among the other candidates.

As I tap on her photo, I feel a spark of excitement. Something about her profile speaks to me, a passion and gentleness that would be perfect for Emily. "What can you tell me about Fräulein Wolff?" I ask Hans.

He pulls up his file with details on her teaching style and experience. "Most reports praise her enthusiasm, creativity, and kindhearted nature. Students describe her as an inspiring teacher who makes learning fun."

I lean back in my chair, steepling my fingers as I consider my options. While she may be less experienced than the other candidates, all signs point to her being a good role model and teacher for Emily. They could learn and grow together. Yes, she seems like the perfect choice.

. . .

"Please contact Fräulein Wolff and schedule a meeting," I instruct Hans. "I feel she will be an excellent match for Emily."

Hans smiles warmly. "A wonderful choice, seine Exzellenz. I will make the arrangements right away."

As he leaves, I look out at the lush gardens below and allow myself to feel hopeful for the first time in a long while. Perhaps this is a new beginning for us after all.

———

Emily hasn't slept all night. She bursts into my study, red-faced and out of breath, clutching her violin case tightly. "Has she come yet? Is she here?" Emily's feet tapping anxiously against the hardwood floor.

I chuckle at her enthusiasm. "Not yet, darling. Be patient. Fräulein Wolff will be here soon."

Emily peers out the window, bouncing on her toes. "Do you think she'll like me? What if I'm not good enough? I've been practicing every day, just like you said."

"You will be wonderful." I rest my hands on her shoulders. "Just be yourself and have fun. That's the most important thing."

• • •

There's a knock at the door and Emily squeals. I straighten my tie and jacket. "Are you ready?"

She nods vigorously, a smile lighting up her face. When the door opens, my breath catches in my throat at the sight of Fräulein Wolff standing there. Wow!

"Guten Tag," she says, curtsying slightly. "I'm Anna Wolff. It's a pleasure to meet you, seine Exzellenz." Beautiful and vibrant, she seems to glow from within. I am mesmerized, struggling to find my words.

"John," I say. "The pleasure is all mine, Fräulein Wolff." I find my eyes lingering on her, drinking every detail. The soft wiggle of her hips as she moves, the gentle curve of her neck, the way strands of hair caress her cheek, and the flattering green dress that accentuates her curves just so. An unfamiliar warmth stirs inside me, awakening parts of myself long dormant. What is this woman doing to me? I clench my jaw, ignoring the burgeoning desire kindling to life. Now is not the time.

Emily is grinning from ear to ear. They leave the room together, Emily chattering a mile a minute. I remain in the study, listening to their fading voices and the stir of desire simmering inside me. I run a hand over my face with a sigh. I am in trouble.

2

ANNA

The taxi approaches the massive iron gates, and my heart leaps. What have I gotten myself into?

"Fraulein, we have arrived." The driver turns around, eyeing me expectantly.

I take a deep, steadying breath and hand him a few bills. "Danke."

The gates swing open silently, and we roll up the winding cobblestone drive. I gasp. The estate is enormous, a sprawling ivory palace with towers and turrets silhouetted against the azure sky.My violin case trembles on my lap; the thought of meeting the American ambassador turns my knees to jelly.

. . .

The cab stops at the entrance, and a suited young man hurries down the steps. I emerge on shaky legs, clutching my violin case like a shield.

"Fraulein Wolff, welcome. I'm Hans, the ambassador's assistant."

"It's a pleasure to meet you, Hans."

"The pleasure is ours. Please." He gestures me up the steps through a pair of towering oak doors. "The ambassador is expecting you in his study," he says politely.

As I step inside, the grand foyer towers over me, my worn heels clicking on the pristine marble floors. My cheap high street coat suddenly feels out of place amidst the opulence of gilded mirrors and a chandelier dripping with crystals. I can't help but feel self-conscious as Hans leads me down a long hallway adorned with expensive artwork. This is not exactly what I am used to. I have to remind myself this is my chance to share my passion for music and perhaps inspire it in another. And the job pays well. VERY well.

I straighten my shoulders and lift my chin, clutching my violin case. We stop before a set of double doors, and Hans knocks. "Seine Exzellenz, Fraulein Wolff has arrived."

The doors swing open to reveal Ambassador John Sinclair himself, just as powerfully compelling as I had imagined.

His sharp blue eyes seem to see right through me, and his chiseled jawline can cut glass.

I dip into a curtsy. "Guten Tag, seine Exzellenz. I am Anna Wolff."

"John," he says swiftly. "This is my daughter, Emily." The ambassador steps aside to reveal a young girl brimming with excitement. She glances up at me with curious green eyes and a bright smile.

"Hello," the little girl says softly. My heart squeezes. She is so precious. I know at once that I will do anything to nurture her gift, to see that smile blossom into joy as she masters a new technique or conquers a difficult passage.

"Emily, say hello properly." The ambassador fixes her with a stern look, though amusement dances in his eyes.

She extends her hand. "Guten Tag, Fraulein Wolff. Welcome." Her German is perfect.

"The pleasure is mine." I cross the room and clasp her hands warmly in mine. "I have been told you have been playing violin for two years. That is wonderful. Music is a gift, and the violin is the finest instrument for channeling passion and creativity."

· · ·

Her cheeks pinken at my praise. "Do you really think so?"

"I know so. The violin has been my greatest joy, and now I can share that joy with you."

She starts firing question after question before taking my hand. "Let me show you my violin," she says, leading me out of the study.

For our first lesson, the ambassador insists on being present. As Emily chatters about the piece, I steal glances at him. He cuts an imposing figure by the fireplace, one hand braced on the mantle, watching us with a softness that belies his sharp features. His waistcoat clings to broad shoulders tapered to a trim waist, and I want to smooth the crease between his brows and trace the strong line of his jaw.

Heat pools low in my belly at the thought, intensifying under his gaze. It's magnetic, like a physical touch that raises gooseflesh along my arms. I imagine those hands, so powerful yet graceful, gliding over my body with the same practiced ease as he signs his name to important documents.

I jerk my attention back to Emily, face flushing. What is wrong with me? I have just met the man, yet I have wholly inappropriate thoughts! He is my employer, a man of status and wealth, and I'm here to do a job. I can't mess this up; I need the money!

. . .

I must maintain a professional distance...but oh, the way he's looking at me makes me want to throw all caution aside.

I clear my throat and focus on Emily. "Shall we begin your lesson?"

Emily nods eagerly, pulling her violin and bow from the case. I arrange my sheet music on the stand as she tunes the instrument. When I glance up, the ambassador has moved to stand by the piano, arms folded over his chest. His gaze holds a challenge that sends a thrill through me.

I wet my lips and face Emily. "We will start with some simple scales to warm up." I guide Emily through the scales, listening for any sour notes. Satisfied with her progress, I move on to a beginner piece by Haydn.

"Keep your wrist straight and elbow high," I say, demonstrating the proper posture. "Draw the bow smoothly across the strings. No jerking motions."

Emily plays the piece with concentration, though not without some mistakes. I give her pointers to help improve her technique, aware of the ambassador's eyes following my every move.

. . .

When Emily finishes, he claps heartily. "Very nicely done, darling."

Emily beams at the praise. I should feel satisfied with a lesson well taught. Still, there's a restlessness inside me that has nothing to do with the violin and everything to do with the man watching us. As Emily puts away her violin, he approaches me. "Thank you, Miss Wolff. I'm impressed with how quickly Emily is progressing under your guidance."

His voice is like aged whiskey, warm and smooth. I stare at his cravat to avoid meeting his eyes. "Emily is a bright student. She simply needs practice and patience."

"As do we all." His fingers brush mine as he takes the sheet music, sending a spark through my skin. "I look forward to her next lesson...and speaking with you further."

My heart flutters at his words. Does he feel this pull between us as strongly as I do? Emily returns, oblivious to the tension hanging in the air. "Are we finished for today?"

I clear my throat. "Yes, that will be all for now. Practice the pieces we went over and be ready to play them for me tomorrow."

"I will." She gathers her things and goes to say goodbye to her father. Alone with the ambassador, the air seems to hum with possibility. He steps closer, and my breath catches.

3

JOHN

The bow glides across the violin strings, releasing a velvet melody into the air. Anna's eyes are closed as she rocks gently, her body attuned to the rhythms. Her cheeks are flushed, lips parted.

I lean against the wall, watching her from the shadows. She's lost in the music, eyes closed, swaying gently. The tune seeps into my bones, as intoxicating as the rose scent of her hair.

I shouldn't be here. Shouldn't be spending so much time with her, my daughter's violin teacher. Attending the first lesson was supposed to be a formality, a way for me to ensure her suitability. Instead, I find myself craving every moment we share, and my fascination with her deepens with each one. She is clever, kind, witty, and well-read, and her passion for music matches mine.

· · ·

I check my watch and sigh. I have a meeting in twenty minutes and a dozen crises to resolve. My daughter Emily will be arriving soon for her lesson.

Anna finishes the piece with a trembling final note. Silence falls, broken only by my ragged breath and heart pounding. She opens her eyes and finds mine. For a moment, she seems startled to see me there. Then a smile lights her face, bright as the Viennese sun. "Herr Ambassador. Back for another lesson?"

I clear my throat, struggling to tamp down my body's reaction to her presence. "You play beautifully, Fräulein Wolff." The words are stilted and formal. A shield to hide behind.

A flicker of disappointment crosses her face before she turns away. I curse myself for being a fool. Why am I pushing her away when all I want is to pull her close?

I grasp for something to rekindle the connection. "Will you join me for a drink sometime?" The words escape before I can stop them.

Anna freezes, her eyes locking onto mine. For a long moment, silence hangs between us, fragile and breakable. Then a smile lights her face, soft and timid. "I would like that very much, Ambassador."

· · ·

"John," I correct her, my heart racing at the sound of my name from her lips. "Call me John."

"John," she repeats, and I can't resist any longer. I close the distance between us in three strides and take the violin from her hands, placing it carefully on the side table. The brief touch ignites a fire that I can no longer contain. I'm hard already.

Propriety be damned. I caress her cheek, and she leans into my touch with a soft sigh, her eyes fluttering closed. I lean in closer "Anna," I whisper.

Her eyes fly open, searching my face. I hold her gaze unflinchingly. She is necessary to me as the air I breathe. After a long moment, she smiles—and takes my hand.

I bend my head and capture her lips. They are soft and plump, like delicate rose petals. The kiss deepens, igniting a fire I never want to extinguish. Her hands tangle in my hair as I deepen the kiss, pulling her soft curves against me. I can feel the heat radiating from her skin as she responds to my hands roaming all over her body, matching my passion with her own.

A loud moan escapes her throat, I can feel my arousal pressing against her stomach, and I know she can feel it, too.

· · ·

This is dangerous. Reckless.

We break apart, breathless, but I keep Anna close, our foreheads touching. Her breaths come as swiftly as my own. Our chests rise and fall against each other. She's my daughter's teacher, and this kiss could complicate everything. My daughter ...

"I shouldn't have done that," I say, though I don't regret it. "My life is ... complicated ... Emily."

"I understand, " she says softly, her hand resting on my chest. I brush a thumb over her kiss-swollen lips before tucking a loose strand behind her ear and ,with one last look, I turn and walk away.

Fool.

4

ANNA

John's lips crash onto mine, his breath hot and demanding. I can taste the hint of mint on his tongue as he kisses me deeply. My heartbeat quickens as his hands tangle in my hair, pulling me closer to him.

I press myself against him, feeling the hard muscles of his chest beneath his shirt. A jolt of desire shoots through me as I melt into his embrace, powerless to resist. His scent washes over me, a mixture of sandalwood and spice that sends shivers down my spine. I run my hands up his back, feeling every inch of his body pressed against mine.

But just as quickly as it began, he pulls away, panting and apologizing. I can see the desire etched into the lines of his face, but he steps back and shakes his head. "I can't...my life is complicated," he mutters before leaving without another word.

．　．　．

I stand there, stunned and confused by his sudden change in demeanor. How could he ignite such passion only to quench it so abruptly? The room is silent except for the sound of my ragged breathing. I touch my swollen lips before Emily's arrival snaps me out of my daze.

"Anna, what's wrong?" she asks, clutching her violin case. "Father seems upset."

I force a smile and brush off her concern. "It's nothing for you to worry about, darling," I say with a tight throat. "Let's start the lesson."

The next day Emily is waiting for me at the door, "Anna! I've been waiting for you all morning."

I force a smile. "My apologies. I had some errands to run before our lesson."

"That's alright." Emily peers at me, her gaze too wise for a nine year-old. "Is something wrong?"

"Of course not," I say briskly. "Shall we begin our lesson?" Emily opens her mouth as if to ask another question. But then she nods and leads me into the music room.

Emily begins Mozart's Sonata in F for Violin and Keyboard, K. 547, her bow gliding effortlessly over the strings. I try to focus on her music, but my mind keeps drifting to her father. Memories of his touch and kisses flood my thoughts, causing a lump in my throat.

Emily finishes the sonata and looks at me expectantly. I can only manage a nod in approval, unable to speak past the lump in my throat. She furrows her brow and asks, "Are you feeling ill, Anna?"

"Just a headache. It's nothing to worry about," I lie.

"We can stop the lesson if you are not feeling well," she offers with concern.

"No, let's continue." I insist. I don't want to cut the lesson short. As painful as it is to be here, these daily meetings with Emily have become a lifeline. I can't give them up so easily.

"Very well." Emily begins another piece, Paganini's Caprice No. 24, her fingers dancing across the strings. But after a few measures, she falters and lowers her violin.

"What's wrong?" I ask.

Emily worries her lip before finally speaking up. "It's my father. Did something happen between you two?"

· · ·

I freeze, caught off guard by her perceptiveness. "Nothing for you to worry about," I reply carefully.

"But it's upsetting you," she insists. "I don't like seeing you so sad."

My throat tightens at her concern. "Your father and I will work through it," I assure her. "In the meantime, let's continue our lesson, alright?"

Emily still looks doubtful. But she lifts her violin again and plays, although her notes lack their usual confidence. I can't let my feelings for John impact Emily. I'll find a way to move past this. For her sake.

The next day, Emily's voice chirps through the phone, inviting me to join her and John for a picnic in the Volksgarten park. "It's such a beautiful day, Fräulein Anna," she says. "Please come with us."

I want to refuse; the thought of seeing John again is both exciting and painful. But I can't deny Emily.

"I would love that," I force a cheer into my tone. "What time shall we meet?"

We arrange to meet at the entrance of the park at noon. I spend the morning battling my emotions, trying to build up defenses for the afternoon ahead. By the time I arrive at the meeting spot, I have convinced myself that I have control over my feelings. Or so I thought.

When I see John standing next to Emily, my heart skips a beat. Our eyes lock for a brief moment. I can see the turmoil in his eyes that mirrors mine, and I must look away.

"Fräulein Anna, you came!" Emily exclaims as she jumps up to wrap her arms around me. I return her hug, taking solace in her warmth.

"Of course," I reply. "A picnic in the Volksgarten is too lovely to miss."

"I'm glad you think so." As he speaks, John's voice is tense; his expression closed off. "Shall we find a spot to sit?" he adds.

We settle near the Theseus Temple and unpack the picnic basket with a sense of unease hanging over us. Emily prattles on, seemingly oblivious to the tension between us. But John's silence weighs heavily on me. It is going to be a long afternoon.

Every day comes a new invitation from Emily to explore a different part of Vienna. The Hofburg Palace, the Burggarten Garden Cafe, the Otto-Wagner Pavillon, and the Belvedere Museum.

. . .

Today, it is the Schönbrunn Palace. "Father has been dying to show you the gardens," Emily says excitedly. "He thinks you'll find them simply fascinating."

Sweet little girl, she is up to something.

5

EMILY & JOHN

The golden sunset light filters through the stained-glass windows, dappling the oak floor in shades of crimson and amber. I pause outside the heavy wooden doors, smoothing my hands over my burgundy dress and taking a deep breath.

It is now or never.

I knock softly and push the doors open. Father looks up from his leather armchair. "Emily, come in."

I perch on the arm of his chair, searching for the right words."Papa, ... I've noticed ... how you look at Anna," I say quietly. "The way your eyes light up when she walks into a room," I pause to look at his reaction. "The smile on your lips when she laughs."

• • •

Father's gaze drops, color rising in his cheeks. "You love her." It isn't a question.

He runs a hand through his ash blonde hair with a sigh. "I didn't mean for it to happen. I tried to fight it, but..." he says.

"But you can't," I finish for him. I take his hand, giving it a gentle squeeze. "Anna is kind, intelligent, loving...she is perfect for you. For us."

Father stares at me, his blue eyes misting. "You...you approve?"

I smile. "With all my heart. You need to make a move, Papa."

"Mein Schatz, you have made me the happiest man alive," he whispers, stroking my hair. I breathe the familiar scent of parchment and pine, content in my father's arms.

———

"I should go find Anna. Tell her how I feel before I lose my nerve."

"Go." Emily gives me a playful shove toward the door. "What are you waiting for?"

• • •

I race through the streets of Vienna, my heart pounding as fast as my feet. Emily's words echo in my mind, freeing me from doubts and giving me wings.

Anna. I have to find Anna. Tell her the truth I can no longer contain.

Her brownstone comes into view, lights glowing in the windows against the velvet night sky. I take the steps two at a time and pound on the door, breathless. When Anna opens the door, the sight of her steals what little air I have left. She is dressed in a pale blue negligee, hair tumbling around her shoulders.

"John?" Surprise colors her voice as she pulls her robe tighter. "What are you doing here at this hour?"

I sweep her into my arms, the softness of her body molding against me. "I'm happy when I am with you and not when you are not with me. You're my heart, my everything, and I don't want to waste another moment pretending other-wise."I whisper fiercely.

Anna gasps, her eyes widening. Before she can speak, I kiss her fiercely. She melts against me with a sigh, her lips parting to deepen the kiss. I kick the door closed and pin her against the wall.

• • •

I lift her thigh around my hip, thrusting deep inside her welcoming heat. No more restrain. Fuck propriety. Anna cries out, nails digging into my back as I begin to move. Her sweet nips and moans fill my ears. I slam into her over and over, driving every desire inside me to the surface.

Her soft gasps echo against my mouth as I undo the clasp of her robe. Her breasts fall free, heavy in my hands, nipples hardened by desire. I groan into her ear, sucking one into my mouth with rough passion. I lift her up, my cock still inside her, and I crash her onto the sofa. I pull her legs up and wide and plunge myself inside her once again like an animal.

"John, oh god...John," she cries out, nails raking my shoulders. A sweet, agonized sound that drives me mad. I bite her earlobe, my hand cupping her breast as I slam my hips into hers, over and over.

"Fuck you feel good, "I say. I want to possess every inch of her. I slide my finger on her clit, feeling it swell under my touch. She cries out, body shuddering in pleasure.

I stand up, pull her with me, and slam my cock into her from behind; she bucks her hips back on me, grinding against my hand now wrapped around her clit. "Anna," I growl, my voice ragged.

"John," she moans as I press on that spot again. Her scream pierces the small apartment as she comes undone in my arms, and I follow quickly after, shooting my seed inside her warmth.

But I want more. I slide down between her legs and begin to eat her pussy, my tongue going to town on her sweet folds. "Oh, John," she cries out with a mixture of pain and pleasure. I lick her slowly and tease her before sliding it into her entrance, sucking hard on her clit.

She screams again, clawing at my head in approval. "So good," she shouts as I lap up the juices of her arousal. My tongue laps at her clit, bringing her another orgasm just as she begins to get a grip.

I pull away, panting and looking into her eyes. "I love you," I say simply.

The rest of the night plays like a blur, and we make love on every surface our bodies can fit on. Finally, sated and sticky sweet, we collapse into bed.

EPILOGUE
ANNA

The golden hues of the setting sun bleed through the grand windows of the Musikverein, bathing the gilded hall in a warm embrace. I lean closer to John, my husband. His hand finds mine, fingers entwining.

"Look at her," I murmur, my gaze transfixed on the small figure taking center stage. Emily in her sapphire dress, cradling her violin like a cherished lover.

John's grip tightens slightly, his thumb caressing the back of my hand. The first notes quivers into existence, Emily's bow dances across the strings.

I close my eyes, allowing the melody to envelop me, to carry me away on its powerful current. The resonance fills the hall, and I feel John's presence beside me, his warmth, his strength.

. . .

Emily's performance reaches its zenith, the final note hanging in the air, pure and exultant. The audience erupts into applause. We rise to our feet, clapping until our hands ache, pride swelling in our chests as we watch Emily takes her bow.

I turn to him, our eyes locking in silent conversation. Love, desire, family - this is our Viennese waltz.

SYDNEY SPARKS

PROLOGUE
DIANE

The scent of the ocean mixed with coconut oil wafts through the airplane as it descends onto the tarmac at Sydney International Airport. My daughter, Sarah, has been begging me to visit for months, promising sun-drenched beaches and a lively nightlife to escape the dreary British weather.

After thirty years of marriage, the divorce papers are signed and sealed. My nest is empty; the business is sold. I'm adrift and alone for the first time, unmoored from everything that once defined me.I take one last look at myself in the compact airplane mirror and adjust my blonde bob.

Stepping off the plane, the intense heat of Australia smacks me in the face. I can't help but smile at the stark contrast to the cold drizzle of home. After going through customs, I spot my daughter Sarah holding a large sign in her hand. The elegant cursive script reads, "Welcome, Mum." We embrace tightly and exchange gentle sniffs, a special mother-daughter tradition.

We drive to Sarah's house, and we catch up over steaming cups of good old Tetley tea. I can't help but smile at the sound of Australian accents bouncing off the walls around me, the little ones are entirely Australian.

I retire early sinking into crisp cotton sheets, exhausted from the long journey. As I lay in bed, the weight of my ex-husband's words and actions weigh heavy on my mind. Images of his younger mistress and our lackluster sex life haunt my thoughts, causing a knot to form in my stomach. Spineless bastard.

After a few weeks of relaxing on the beach and indulging in good food, I crave something more. Something adventurous that will make me feel alive again. I yearn for adventure.

1

———

DIANE

I step onto the yacht, my heels click against the glossy deck, and the smell of sea salt fills my nostrils, my first solo outing. The sun beats down on me as I take in the sparkling Sydney Harbor. Electronic music pulsates through the yacht, and I feel the vibrations beneath my feet.

As I sip on my champagne, I scan the crowd of tanned, toned bodies half my age until my gaze snags on a pair of intense blue eyes gazing straight at me from across the deck. A shiver runs down my spine as a slow, knowing smile spreads across his ruggedly handsome face.

Everything about this man screams alpha: from his broad shoulders filling out a white linen shirt to the commanding way he strides through the crowd toward me, people parting before him. My heart races and a wave of desire washes over me as he stops before me, his eyes never leaving mine, a feeling I haven't known in years.

• • •

"Beautiful, isn't it?" he says in a deep, rumbling voice that stirs me.

"It is," I say, my mouth suddenly dry. I grip the rail, acutely aware of his sculpted arms and broad shoulders. A tingling sensation spreads through my body at the thought of how those muscles would feel against my skin. His gaze travels the length of my body in a slow, scorching sweep that makes my pulse race.

"I'm Liam." He extends a calloused hand. "Welcome to my yacht, Ms...?"

"Diane." I place my hand in his, and his fingers tighten, holding me fast.

"A pleasure to meet you, Diane." His voice is a low rumble, his eyes gleaming with heat and promise. "What's a stunning woman like yourself doing here, alone?"

My cheeks flush at the compliment. It's been long since a man looked at me this way. "Just visiting my daughter," I say, struggling to steady my voice. Why did I say that? God is young; he could be around her age.

"How about you, Liam? What do you do when you're not hosting lavish parties?"

· · ·

A wry smile tugs at his lips. "I'm a sailor. I go where the wind and tides take me." His thumb grazes the back of my hand, sending a delicious shiver down my spine. "And right now, they're taking me to you."

I open my mouth, but before I can respond, he brings my hand to his lips. The brush of his mouth against my skin sends a spark through me.

"Would you care to see my yacht?" Liam asks, a promise in his eyes. As I look up at him, I am met with an intense gaze filled with desire and longing. His eyes seem to see directly into my soul, making me feel both vulnerable and powerful at the same time. The air between us is thick, and I must take a long, deep breath to steady myself.

"I'd love to." The words are out before I can think as if this man has some magnetic pull on me. I'm powerless to resist.

He leads me through the deck, his hand holding mine until he stops at the deserted stern and pulls me close. Our bodies are pressed together on the rail; I can feel the hardness of his erection against me. A gasp escapes my lips at the sensation, and I instinctively grind against him for more. He wraps an arm around my waist, pulling me even closer to him.

I swallow hard, torn between propriety and desire. "We barely know each other."

• • •

"I know enough." His gaze smolders. "I know you're not like the others. You have fire in you, passion—you just need someone to ignite it."

His words strike a chord deep within me. I want to protest but can't find the words. Can't think at all with his scent enveloping me, sandalwood and sea.

"You smell so fucking good," he murmurs into my skin.

Oh God, I am so turned on. "Thank you," I whisper back like a shy little girl, my breath hot against his mouth.

He pulls back to look at me, his eyes burning with desire, a grin that tugs at his lips. "You're welcome," he says slowly, his voice thick with lust. He leans in again, lips hovering just millimeters from mine. The heat between us is unbearable.

I've never felt so desired before. Our lips finally touch. His are soft yet firm, demanding. His tongue teases at my lips, and I open them for him, eager for more. His hand slides up my spine, cupping the nape of my neck, pulling me even closer. It feels so taboo but freeing, so right.

My hands roam over his strong arms and chest, feeling the muscles ripple beneath his shirt. With each movement, the heat between us intensifies until it's all-consuming. Liam's hands move lower, cupping my buttocks and pulling me flush against him.

What am I doing? "I could be your mother, " I say, trying to pull away.

"I never wanted to fuck my mother..." he growls, holding me close. "I want you, Diane."

My eyes flutter shut. "Here?" I rasp.

"I don't care." His hands slide under my dress, calloused palms skimming up my thighs.

"Anyone could see."

"My cabin, then," and he takes me below deck.

The cabin door slams behind us. Liam pushes me against the wall and strips off; his cock springs free - huge and hard against his muscular thighs. Oh, Jesus.

"Like what you see?" A wicked grin tugs at his lips. He steps closer, bracketing me with his arms. The empty void within me, the restless longing I've lived with for so long, begins to fade. In its place blooms a singular desire, all-consuming and desperate.

. . .

"I'm going to make you mine now, Diane." His hands slide under my dress again, nudging it over my hips. Then, they slide down to grip my thighs, spreading them open. I want more than anything to be taken by him.

"Fuck me, "I say. I can't believe I said that. "I need you."

"Say it again," he orders.

"I need you." This time, it's a confession more than a plea.

He steps closer, guiding it to my wetness before pressing the head against my opening. I am so wet I am soaking.

"You feel so good," he mumbles against my skin as he slides in slowly. I can feel every inch of him claiming me. My walls stretch to accommodate him. He pounds on me, hammering me to the wall, and his body claps against mine. It feels so good, better than anything I've ever known.

"Oh fuck," I moan loudly.

His hands grip my hips, pulling me closer to him as he thrusts harder.

. . .

"You're mine," he declares, deep groans filling the cabin.

"Yes," I gasp, clinging to him. "Fuck me harder." Who am I?

I brace myself on the wall as the pleasure consumes me, washing over me like a wave. Liam grows rougher, his hips pounding faster, pushing deeper inside of me. It feels perfect. He slams into me hard, filling that void within me, claiming every inch of my body for his own pleasure.

2

LIAM

The salty breeze kisses my skin as I steer the yacht around the harbor, admiring how the setting sun ignites the rippling waves with shades of pink and orange. Diane stands at the bow, her hair dancing in the wind, a smile of pure bliss on her lips.

My cock swells at the sight of her, my heart pounding. Each day we spend together, she grows bolder and more at ease in her own skin. There's a sensuality to her movements now, an uninhibited grace I find irresistible. She a real woman. My woman now.

"Take us out to the open sea," she says, facing me. Her eyes glint with mischief. "I want to feel the waves."

Heat coils in my gut at her bold request. "As you wish."

. . .

I steer us out of the harbor until the yacht crests the swells of the sea. Diane shrieks in delight, her arms spread wide. The motion causes her dress to ride up her thighs, revealing smooth, tanned skin that makes my mouth water.

Unable to resist, I join her at the bow, pulling her against me. Her body molds to mine as if made for me. "You're so beautiful like this," I murmur, nuzzling her neck. "Free. Wild."

She tilts her head to the side, baring the long line of her throat. "You make me feel that way."

I groan, seized by a sudden, fierce need to possess her, to show her how I feel the only way I know how. I scoop her into my arms and carry her below deck to the cabin.

I waste no time stripping her bare, feasting on each inch of her skin. Her soft moans and whispered pleas spur me on as I worship her body, staking my claim in the most primal way I know.

When, at last, we join, the world falls away. There is only Diane, her body fused with mine, my cock inside her. This is all I need.

3

DIANE

Sarah folds her arms, her eyes stormy. "Mom, this has gone too far. You're not thinking straight."

I run my fingers over the soft fabric of the silk robe that Liam gave me, feeling warmth rise in my cheeks, "I'm perfectly capable of making my own decisions."

"You're making a fool of yourself for some 'boy toy'?" Her voice grows shrill with judgment.

Anger flickers in my chest. "Liam is not a boy, just like you are not a girl anymore. He is a man. A strong, passionate man who appreciates me for who I am." I never told her about her spineless father, his digs, his betrayal.

· · ·

She scoffs at my words. "He is just using you for sex," she accuses, "and when he gets tired of you, he'll dump you for someone younger."

My temper flares; I am angry now; how dare she? "Maybe I'm using HIM for sex," I retort. "Ever thought about that?"

"Mother!!!" she says in shock. She has always been a prude and restrained like her father. "He's near my age! What will people say?"

I bristle. "I don't care what people say," I answer firmly. "Liam makes me happy. He cares about me, and that's all that matters."

"Does he really? Did he bother telling you that he plans to leave soon to sail around the world? Did he ask you to go with him?"

My heart drops, but I refuse to let it show. Yes, his sailing trip. I remember him mentioning it once before, "Oh, just some solo sailing for a year or so," he said casually. It didn't mean anything then, but now my heart is aching. We've only just begun, and soon he'll be leaving. A year is a long time.

But I refuse to let it show. "He does not owe me any explanation. We are having fun. Fun, remember that?" I rebut instead.

. . .

"I can't believe you're choosing him over your family," Sarah says, her voice thick with tears. It's a familiar tactic of hers - guilt-tripping me when things don't go her way.

I reach for her hands. "Sweetheart, I'm not choosing him over you. But you have your life, your family, and I must live mine."

"If you continue with this, you'll regret it." She jerks away from me and storms out of the room, slamming the door behind her.

I sink onto the sofa, throat tight, but all I can think of is seeing him again ...

4

LIAM

My breath hitches as the sun sets over the horizon, casting a warm glow on Diane's skin. She's lying on her back on the deck of my yacht, her eyes closed, enjoying the last rays of the day's light. She's wearing one of my oversized t-shirts that barely covers her bottom, showing off her slender legs and that perfect ass.

Every curve and inch of her body has become my obsession - from the tiny wrinkles around her eyes to the softness of her stomach and those plump lips that tremble slightly when she moans.

I take a slow sip of whiskey, savoring the smoothness of it.

The smell of saltwater and sunscreen fills my lungs, making me dizzy with desire. I step closer to her, feeling the warmth radiating from her body.

. . .

Slowly, I kneel beside her, our legs brushing against each other. She doesn't stir, too lost in her own world. A soft sigh escapes her lips, and I lean closer, pressing my side against hers. Desire courses through my veins like a drug. My fingers trace along her jawline, causing her to moan softly. It's the sexiest sound I've ever heard.

"You're so beautiful," I whisper against her ear, flicking my tongue against the lobe. "Do you know how many times I think about this?"

Her breath catches in her throat, and she tilts her head back, exposing her neck to me. "What do you think about?" she breathes out.

"About how you feel under me, how you taste," I reply, pulling her closer so our bodies are pressed together.

I lean in and claim her lips in a heated kiss, tasting the sweet wine on her tongue.

"Come, "I say, taking her hand and leading her toward the lower deck before I make love to her right here in front of everyone.

Below deck, I push her onto the bed and trail kisses down her jawline, over her collarbone, stopping at the edge. I pull the t-shirt over her head, revealing perfect breasts swaying gently with each movement. They are soft and full in my hands, their rosy nipples hardening under my touch. The scent of her arousal fills my nostrils as I take one nipple into my mouth, sucking it greedily. She gasps, and I suckle harder, rolling it between my tongue and teeth. Her hands grip my hair, holding me tightly as she arches her back, urging me on.

"Liam," she moans.

My hand finds its way to her ass cheek, squeezing gently before trailing up her thigh, my erection pressing into her. My fingers move to her panties, pushing them down slowly, inch by inch.

I step back to admire the view, my cock throbbing in anticipation. She's beautiful, her body glowing in the soft light. I kneel before her, my lips moving downwards, kissing and licking her thighs before parting her folds with my fingers. I inhale her musky scent, my tongue darting out to taste her.

She arches off the bed with a loud moan as my tongue flicks against her sensitive entrance. I slip a finger inside her, savoring how wet and tight she feels around me. She grinds against my face, begging for more.

"Fuck," she breathes, her voice ragged.

• • •

I stand up, my thick shaft pressing against her entrance. I position myself, pushing inside her slowly, filling her up inch by hot, tight inch. She gasps sharply as I finally penetrate.

"You're mine," I murmur, starting a slow, deep rhythm. She comes first, crying out my name. I follow soon after, collapsing on top of her, panting heavily.

I hold her tightly, not wanting this moment to end. I want to spend the rest of my days like this, fucking her, holding her in my arms. I can't lose her. "Come with me. Let's explore the world together," I blurt out. I'm not a great talker.

The yacht gently rocks beneath us, water lapping against the hull, providing a soothing rhythm to the moment.

She bites her lip, making me ache for her even more. "Liam..." she whispers.

I hold my breath as I wait for her response."Say yes."

5

DIANE

The sun's last rays stretch across the horizon, the sky a canvas of pinks, oranges, and purples. The water glistens with the reflection of the sinking sun, creating a pathway of light that leads out to the endless ocean. The salty tang of the sea air fills my nostrils with hints of seaweed and sunscreen. I can taste it on my lips.

Liam stands behind me on the beach, his arms wrapped around my waist. Bora Bora, our latest stop. I lean against him, feeling his strong muscles and warmth seeping through my skin. His lips gently brush against my temple. He makes me feel so alive.

"It's beautiful," I say, gazing at the horizon.

"It is," he agrees. "Just like you."

• • •

I turn in his arms to face him, and smile as the last light of day disappears.

"You always know just what to say," I murmur. I never felt more beautiful and more desired in my entire life.

"I have plenty more compliments if you want," he teases. I feel a familiar heat building in my core at his touch.

"Flattery will get you everywhere," I reply.

His hands slide down to rest on my hips before trailing upwards to gently cup my breasts through my bikini top. Bikini! Who am I? A surge of heat rushes through me at his touch, and I instinctively melt into him, seeking more of his caresses.

"You're insatiable," he murmurs, nuzzling into my neck with soft kisses.

"Only for you," I respond without hesitation. And it is true.

In Liam's arms, I am free. This is as real as it gets. As the sun sets on this paradise beach, I know this is precisely where I'm meant to be - with him.

AMSTERDAM AFFAIR

1

———————

EMILY

The cobblestone streets of Amsterdam greet me like an old friend as I step off the plane. I've always loved this city, its quaint cafes lining the canals and historic charm around every corner. As a travel writer, I'm here on assignment to explore the museums and soak in the culture, but it feels more like coming home. Fourteen days to heaven.

After checking into my cozy hotel nestled along one of the central canals, I head straight for the Rijksmuseum. My heart races as I walk through the arched entryway, taking in the musty scent of oil paintings and marble sculptures. I breeze past the more famous works, my sights set on finding the hidden gems that tell Amsterdam's unique story. But then I stop.

Rembrandt's The Night Watch, the museum's largest and most important work, glowers at me from the canvas, its dark intensity daring me to look away. I won't. I can't. I feel the need to immerse myself in it.

. . .

"Intimidating, isn't it?" The deep voice at my shoulder makes me jump. I whip around to find an impossibly tall man with sharp cheekbones and glacial blue eyes studying me. I'm momentarily speechless as our eyes lock, the air between us crackling with electricity.

"I wasn't aware the paintings had personal bodyguards." The retort escapes before I can rein it in.

His mouth quirks. "Thijs. I'm one of the curators here." He holds out a long-fingered hand.

I take it reluctantly. "Emily."

"American?"

My hackles rise at his peremptory tone. "What gave it away, my loud voice and poor fashion sense?"

He blinks, then lets out a surprised laugh. "Touché. My apologies for the assumption."

"Apology accepted." I turn back to the Rembrandt, acutely aware of Thijs hovering behind me. "I find the darkness beautiful," I muse. "Full of mystery."

. . .

"And passion," Thijs adds quietly. "Rembrandt poured his wild heart onto the canvas for all to see."

I shiver at the image, my writer's mind spinning with fantasies of fierce desire and tangled limbs in shadowy rooms. Thijs steps closer, and suddenly, I'm out of air.

We begin debating the merits of various paintings, parrying thoughts and insights like fencers on the dueling ground. He's intelligent and passionate, with a magnetic pull I can't resist. I've never felt such an instant connection, which unsettles me; his probing eyes and honeyed voice evoke sensations I thought long buried. I need to leave now before I do something reckless.

But he glances at his watch. "I'm afraid I must be going. I'll see you soon," he says, his eyes gleaming with promise. And then he is gone.

"I'll see you soon?" I mutter as I watch his retreating figure. What? I try to refocus on the paintings, but my thoughts keep drifting back to Thijs. His passion for art mirrors mine, yet he seems to guard his true self behind an aloof facade.

I'm jarred from my musings when I realize the museum will close soon. Reluctantly, I make my way toward the exit, casting one final glance over my shoulder at the Rembrandt that started it all.

· · ·

Outside, I'm enveloped by the din of Amsterdam's streets. The crisp evening air helps clear my head as I weave through the crowds. This assignment is meant to be about the artwork, not some intriguing stranger.

When I arrive at the cozy bar near my hotel, my breath catches as I spot Thijs sitting alone at a corner table. He waves me over, eyes glinting in the low light.

"I hoped I'd see you here," he says softly, "Sit." Not an invite, a command. What an arrogant man! But I can't resist and sit across from him, my pulse quickening.

I have a feeling this will be a night I'll never forget...This assignment just got a whole lot more interesting.

2

THIJS

The museum's polished white marble floors gleam under the bright lights, reflecting the warm hues of the paintings on the walls and casting a soft glow throughout the atrium. The air is filled with hushed murmurs as visitors mill around, their clothes a blend of muted colors that add to the elegant atmosphere. And then I see her.

My eyes are immediately drawn to her, standing before the grandeur of Rembrandt's masterpiece, The Night Watch, like a goddess in front of her temple.

I drink in every detail: lush black hair tumbled over pale shoulders, framing a delicate face with full pink lips and high cheekbones. Her emerald eyes sparkle with life, captivating anyone who dares to look into them. Full breasts and hips hint at a womanly figure hidden beneath ill-fitted American clothes, and her skin is smooth and creamy like fresh cream. I can feel a wild spirit hidden beneath a proper facade.

I feel a surge of possessiveness and desire—I want her. Need her.

I approach her, unable to resist. As I talk to her, I feel my control slipping away. If I stay a minute longer, I will unravel before her.

Control yourself, Thijs.

I turn abruptly, pretending to have an urgent meeting. But even as I walk away, I cannot banish her image from my mind, no matter how hard I try. An American tourist, so far beneath me in society, I crave her with an intensity beyond reason.

I have to see her again.

It takes me little time to discover where she is staying. I wait pulse racing in the small bar near the hotel where she is staying. I savor the moment I see her again. I spot her as soon as she passes by, and I gesture her over.

"Join me for a drink." My voice is strained, harsh. "Sit." It is more a command than a request.

· · ·

She hesitates before taking the seat across from me. I drink in the sight of her up close—the curve of her lips, the wayward tendrils of hair. I ache to possess every inch of her. We speak of inconsequential things, but the air between us hums. She is a siren calling to my inner darkness, threatening to breach the walls of generations of proper breeding and restraint.

I gesture to the window, where lights twinkle outside. "Amsterdam has many hidden charms beyond the obvious tourist traps. Let me show you."

She raises an eyebrow in question. "Why would you do that for a stranger?"

"Sometimes fate brings people together for a purpose," I reply, my voice low and intense. "And I feel ours has only just begun."

She accepts my invite and the following day I lead her into the bustling city streets. Our arms brush with each step, and sparks fly between us. I want nothing more than to pull her into a secluded alleyway and taste her exquisite lips. Her quick wit and fiery spirit pull me in even further as we talk. She is a mystery I am desperate to unravel.

The temperature drops as the sun sinks below the horizon and Emily shivers. I quickly remove my coat and drape it around her shoulders, gently rubbing her arms to warm her up. She looks at me with wide eyes but doesn't pull away from my touch.

We come to a stop beside a misty canal. The fading light illuminates her face, more lovely than any work of art. God, she is so beautiful. I reach out and caress her cheek, unable to resist, "Emily..." I breathe her name like a prayer.

She trembles under my touch but does not retreat. The walls between us are crumbling fast. I have to have her. She is meant to be mine.

I pull her close to me, my heart hammering with desire. Our lips meet in a passionate kiss, and I can feel myself losing all control. Emily responds eagerly, tangling her fingers in my hair as I deepen the embrace hungrily. I am drowning in her, losing all reason. She is everything I never knew I needed.

When we finally break apart for air, her cheeks are flushed, and her eyes are filled with longing. "We shouldn't...this is..." she stammers.

I silence her protests with another kiss. "Don't fight this," I whisper against her lips. My hands roam her curves, eliciting soft gasps from her. She clutches onto my shoulders as her knees buckle beneath her. I hold her tight, supporting her weight.

. . .

"Let me take you back to the hotel," I murmur, trailing kisses down her neck. She shivers in response; I know she wants this just as much as I do.

"Thijs..." my name, a breathy sigh on her lips. Hearing her say it nearly undoes me.

"Come ..." I take her hand and lead her away from the bustling canal. She hesitates only for a moment before following me.

I know she is meant to be mine. The way she fits perfectly against my body tells me that we are meant to be together. And nothing will stop me from making her mine. Propriety be damned, she will be mine. She is meant for me.

3

EMILY

My mind is a whirlwind of confusion, desire, and conflict as I try to ignore the throbbing ache between my thighs. I can't afford to lose focus on my writing assignment and get behind.

Yet, every time our bodies brush against each other as we explore the hidden gems of Nieuwe Spiegelstraat or gaze at the historic De Waag, I'm transported to another world where only his touch and presence matter. And despite my efforts to resist, every nerve in my body longs for him.

I hesitate, knowing I shouldn't. After all, I'll only be here for a few more days. I hardly know anything about him. I ... Fuck.

Thijs leads me to my hotel room, his hand on the small of my back, our bodies touching. We enter my hotel room, both knowing what's about to happen. The air thickens with tension, and we no longer bother with pretenses. Thijs locks the door behind him and presses me against it, gripping my hips possessively. His fingers tangle in my hair, pulling slightly as he explores every inch of my mouth with his tongue.

I squirm like a little girl when he cups my breast over the flimsy fabric of my bra, teasing my nipple through the thin material. Shit, why didn't I bring something sexy?

My breath comes in ragged gasps as I plead for more. He deftly undoes the clasp of my bra, and a rush of cool air hits my sensitive skin. His fingers trace circles around my now-erect nipple, sending waves of pleasure through me. I moan as he takes it into his mouth, gently sucking and teasing me. Shit.

I tug at his pants, desperate to feel him inside me. He groans, already hard and eager against the fabric. He steps out of his clothes and pulls off his boxers. I take him in my hand, stroking him slowly as he steps closer to me.

With a low growl, he pushes my legs apart and enters me with a single thrust. It's painful yet exquisite, stretching me in ways I never thought possible. His hips move in a rhythm that matches the rapid beats of my heart.

"You feel soo good, baby, " he growls as he kisses my neck while thrusting deeper and harder, claiming me as his own. I can feel every inch of him inside of me, filling me up completely. His grip tightens on my hips as he picks me up, pressing me against the wall. My legs wrap around him instinctively as he pumps into me with abandon. I cry, feeling the heat building inside me. Oh God!

"Thijs ... pleeeease," I beg for release.

"Not yet, little girl .... not yet." He pulls out abruptly and turns me around, spreading my butt cheeks apart, and I can feel his big hard cock pushing in.

"Ttt...hh... it hu.."

"Shh," he murmurs and presses in, his hand between my legs, fingers pumping in and out as he continues to ravage me.

"Fuck, fuck, fuuuuuuuck," I scream in pleasure as I climax, and soon after, I feel his warm release dripping down my ass.

"Jij bent van mij, kleine meid," he growls possessively in Dutch. It's so sexy, even if I haven't got a clue what he just said.

"What?"I ask breathlessly.

• • •

"You are mine, baby girl," he clarifies with a grin. He's unlike any man I've ever met before—alpha, possessive, demanding, rough yet cultured, with a sophistication of other times, mysterious.

My head spins from the intensity of it all; what am I doing? This man is not someone I can have a future with. I try to pull away, but he holds me close, refusing to let go. "We can't keep doing this," I say weakly.

"We don't have to," he responds, stroking my hair gently. "We can stop whenever you want."

But deep down, I don't want to stop, despite the inevitable heartbreak that awaits me when my time here is up. I crave more of the intense passion that he brings out in me. I want more of him. The only problem is: so does he.

4

EMILY

I pull the zipper of my worn suitcase with a screech, sealing away the memories of our time together. My heart clenches at the thought of leaving him behind. I don't want to leave. Don't want to leave him.

Thijs.

For fourteen magical days, we have been inseparable. He has opened his world to me - art galleries filled with masterpieces, cozy cafes where we shared lattes and sweet pastries, moonlit gondola rides under ancient bridges, and long walks through quiet piazzas. He's been by my side, guiding me, making me laugh, eyes twinkling as he watches my reactions to everything. Fucking me senseless.

I have fallen for him. Hard.

But reality is calling me back to my responsibilities and a life halfway across the globe. His world is here. I swallow hard as tears prick my eyes, knowing I must say goodbye to my Amsterdam love affair.

A sharp knock at the door jolts me out of my thoughts. I know it's him. I take a deep breath and open the door.

And there he is, standing in front of me with flushed cheeks and burning eyes: Thijs, the man who consumes me. Before I can even utter a word, his lips are on mine, crushing and desperate. I feel weak as he sweeps me into his arms and takes me toward the bed.

"I want you," he says between heated kisses.

My pulse races. He wants me. He just wants me. But I want him too, even if only for one last night. He takes me repeatedly, in every way imaginable, as if trying to hold onto me forever.

The clock begins to chime at midnight.

"Don't go," he whispers as we lay tangled in each other's arms. "Stay with me. I love you, Emily."

Tears well up in my eyes at his words, the very thing I've longed to hear from him for so long. "I have a job to return to, "I say instead.

· · ·

"Then I come with you," he declares.

I'm taken aback. Did I hear him correctly? "But what about your job at the museum?" I ask.

He takes a long, deep breath and says. "There's something I need to tell you. I'm not who you think I am."

Confusion clouds my expression. "What do you mean?"

Gently, he takes my hand in his. "My family is one of the oldest aristocratic lines in the country. The museum is just a hobby for me."

I stare at him in shock. Of all the things I expected him to say, this wasn't it.

"Why didn't you ever tell me?" I ask.

His fingers trace patterns on the back of my hand. "I didn't want things to change between us. I just wanted to be Thijs. I wanted you to see me."

He's right.

• • •

"There are obligations that come with my name and position. If you want to be with me, that is?" he asks, searching my eyes for an answer.

I nod vigorously.

"Emily Van der Mert," he says with a grin. "It has a nice ring to it." And then he adds the words that take my breath away.

"Marry me?"

EPILOGUE

THIJS

I 'm seated at the head of the table, watching as Emily glides through the grand dining hall. Our ancestral home is alive with laughter and music; she stands out like a queen. Her gown hugs her curves, drawing everyone's eyes. Tonight is our fifth wedding anniversary, and I am more in love than ever. I can't help but stare at how her hips sway - a sight I can never grow accustomed to and never fails to take my breath away.

As she approaches, I stand up, my hand outstretched to greet her, and she takes it without hesitation.

Her skin is warm against mine, "My love," I whisper, pulling her close. "You are more beautiful tonight than ever." I lean down and kiss her neck softly, breathing in her delicate scent. It's intoxicating, like jasmine and vanilla. Her body presses against mine, and my cock hardens immediately.

· · ·

Emily tilts her head back to look at me, a small smile on her lips. "And you are as handsome as ever." She tastes like wine and promises as our mouths meet in a kiss. We're pulled apart by the sudden hush that falls over the room. Everyone is watching us, waiting for us to sit.

The servants scurry around us, setting out plates of exquisite food and filling glasses with fine wine. But all I can focus on is the rustle of her gown against my trousers and the soft laughter that escapes her lips.

Our eyes never stray far from each other's throughout the meal. Now and then, she shoots me a mischievous glaze. Her fingers graze my thigh under the table, sending chills down my spine. I am a bewitched, body, mind, and soul.

The music starts, and we rise to dance. Her body fits perfectly against mine, and I know she was made for me. My hands glide over the curves of her back, hugging her close as we move together in perfect rhythm. Her soft gasps echo in my ear, and the feel of her breasts pressing against my chest makes me ache.

She is my world, and I am hers.

Emily leans into me, her cheek pressed against my chest. "Thank you for organizing this," she whispers.

· · ·

I couldn't have planned a more perfect evening if I tried. All of this for her, and all that remains is to make her mine. "You're welcome. Now, let's go somewhere more private," I murmur huskily, pulling her away from the crowd.

In the corridor, I push her against a small recess in the corner. Emily giggles as I wrap my arms around her waist, pulling her close. Her laughter is like a siren's song, and I can't resist its call. I trail kisses down her neck, feeling her shiver beneath my touch. I slide my hand up her thigh; she gasps when I reach her core, already wet and ready for me.

I devour her mouth again before climbing up the grand staircase. We enter the bedroom, and she kicks the door shut with her heel. It's dimly lit, and she turns to face me, her eyes full of need. I kick off my shoes, falling to my knees before her. My tongue darts out, tracing the lace of her corset. I can hardly wait to feel her skin against mine. My fingers fumble with the laces, desperate to free her. Her breath hitches as I reveal more of her perfect body with each tug.

Finally, the corset falls away, revealing her creamy skin, and my mouth crashes onto her breasts. I taste her nipples hardening in my mouth.

She grips my hair tightly as I slip off her dress, leaving her in silk stockings and garters. My fingers tracing every inch of her body, making her shiver.

•   •   •

I cup her face gently, then roughly, pulling her closer. She bites her lower lip as I tug at her panties playfully.

Finally free, I taste her, teasing her folds with my tongue, making her gasp. She tastes like heaven, and I'm addicted. I thrust inside of her, feeling her walls grip me tightly.

The bed creaks underneath us, and her nails dig into my shoulders, drawing blood. I love the pain. It only fuels my desire. She meets my every thrust, reaching her climax, crying out my name. I follow soon after, filling her with my seed.

Laying beside her, I stare into her eyes, still trying to catch my breath. She's mine. She always has been, and she always will be.

CAPE TOWN SAFARI

1

CLAIRE

The blaring alarm shatters the silence and jerks me awake. I groggily reach out and slam my hand on the clock, silencing its incessant beeping: another day, another dollar. The thought fills me with a sense of deep weariness and resignation.

With a heavy sigh, I drag myself out of bed and shuffle to the bathroom. I avoid looking in the mirror; it's become a painful reminder of what I've lost. The dark circles under my eyes are a constant companion, proof of how my passionless life is slowly draining my spirit.

Work. Home. Sleep. Repeat. It's a never-ending cycle that feels suffocating and meaningless.

Ever since the divorce, my world has narrowed to this dreary loop. I pour everything into my photography, chasing the next exotic locale, the next rare species to capture on film. My shots grace the pages of all the top nature magazines now. I'm at the peak of my career, yet I've never felt so empty.

This can't be all there is. There must be more. I yearn for the fire I once had, for something real and raw to make me feel alive again. Memories of the past flood my mind as I sit in front of my computer screen, scrolling through old photos and journal entries. I long for the rush of adrenaline that once consumed me, the feeling of truly being alive.

Adventure used to pump through my veins, but now my blood runs cold. I've locked my heart in a cage, too afraid of being hurt to let anyone in. But I'm the one hurting myself most by playing it safe.

No more. I want to break free, even if it terrifies me. I need to get back in touch with my wild side.

My fingers tap furiously on the keyboard, browsing through travel websites. Suddenly, an image catches my eye - a breathtaking photo of a lioness basking in the golden sunset. My heart races, and I can practically taste the adventure in the air. And just like that, I'm hooked. It's time to break free ...

My hands tremble as I click "Purchase Ticket" on the website. A surge of exhilaration rushes through me. I've just booked a two-week photo safari in Klein Karoo, a few hours outside Cape Town. My mind swirls with excitement and fear as I imagine myself surrounded by untamed nature and wild animals - a chance to feel alive again, to reconnect with my passion.

A confirmation email appears in my inbox, I take a deep breath and smile. This is really happening.

I lean back in my desk chair, heart hammering. Doubt creeps in. I've never done anything this impulsive before. I plan every detail of my trips, obsessing over logistics for months. Yet here I am, jumping into the unknown.

Breathe, Claire. This is what you need—a jolt to your system. Out there, surrounded by the rawness and unpredictability of the bush, you'll rediscover your fire.

And you never know who you might meet along the way. A kindred spirit, perhaps. And maybe, just maybe, a man strong enough ... someone who appreciates your strength and independence yet still makes you feel protected... One can only dream...

This trip marks a new chapter. I can feel it in my soul. The Claire who returns will be different from the woman sitting here now. My bags are already packed in my mind. I'm ready for this adventure—good bye New York, Cape Town here I come.

2

CLAIRE

The jeep jolts to a stop, sending me lurching forward in my seat. I steady myself with a hand on the hot metal door frame and squint against the blinding sun as I step out. The dry heat of the African savannah hits me hard, making my skin prickle and my throat parch.

I take in the rustic lodge, its thatched roof blending into the rugged landscape. This is precisely the kind of adventure I have been craving. As if on cue, a tall, muscular figure emerges from the largest building, blonde hair glinting in the sunlight as he strides towards me. With each crunch of his boots on the dusty ground, I can see the coiled strength in his shoulders and arms.

My heart pounds as I can't tear my eyes away from him. Ex-military, no doubt about it. Around my age. He exudes strength and confidence with every move, and I can't help but feel a twinge of excitement mixed with nerves.

· · ·

"Welcome to the bush, Claire," he says in a deep voice with a distinct Afrikaans accent. A shiver runs down my spine at the sound. Those words make it all so real - I am really here, in Africa. And this man named Luke is going to be my private guide for the next two weeks.

His piercing blue eyes meet mine, and I feel he can see straight through to my core. I suddenly feel exposed and vulnerable under his intense gaze.

"Th-thanks," I stutter, mentally cursing myself for suddenly feeling like a flustered schoolgirl. I came here to prove that I'm still an adventurous woman, but in front of this commanding man, I feel small and vulnerable.

A slow smile spreads across his face, "Don't worry, Claire. You're safe with me." A thrill courses through me at the blatant possessiveness in his tone. I want nothing more than to give in to his touch and let him take control. But as excitement fills me, so does a familiar fear - the fear of losing myself in someone else's desires.

"We'll be leaving first thing tomorrow morning. Sleep well," he says firmly.

I settle into my luxurious tented lodge, surrounded by striking rock formations and a breathtaking landscape. The spacious lounge boasts a stylish, contemporary interior and opens to a wooden deck that makes the most of the superb setting. The accommodation is luxurious and private, with an en-suite bathroom and a private patio with a heated plunge pool. As much as I crave adventure and the call of the wild, my days of rough backpacking are long gone.

Bang bang ...

My eyes snap open, and my heart races as I scramble out of bed, still half-asleep. Shit, I have overslept, and a pang of panic shoots through me. As I reach for the door, Luke's tall silhouette blocks the way. "Wakey, wakey," he teases, his eyes sparkling as they roam over my body.

Instinctively, I clutch my nightgown tighter around my body, feeling self-conscious in front of his chiseled physique. But his hungry gaze tells me that none of it matters to him.

"We leave in 30 minutes," he informs me before turning away.

We set out into the bush in Luke's sturdy 4x4; the savannah unfolds before us in all its wild majesty. The sun beats down as we scan the horizon for glimpses of wildlife.

"There's a pride of lions not far from here," Luke says, one hand casually draped over the steering wheel. "If we're lucky, we'll spot them hunting."

· · ·

My heart races at the thought. This rugged landscape awakens something primal within me, a part of myself I didn't know existed until now. Luke glances at me, a knowing smile on his lips. "You'll be hooked after your first sighting," he says confidently. "The bush gets under your skin."

"I can feel it already," I confess; I can't deny the exhilaration coursing through my veins.

His eyes darken, and he reaches across to clasp my hand. "I knew you were meant for this place the moment I saw you."

His words make my breath catch. Part of me wants to pull away and retreat into my shell, but I can't resist his touch. As dusk falls, we make camp beneath endless stars. Luke builds a crackling fire, the flickering light dancing over his rugged features. The chill in the air seeps into my bones, but I'm too entranced by Luke to care. I am shivering.

Luke wraps his arms around me like iron bands, possessive yet tender. "Feeling warmer now?" he asks.

I nod, and I can't help but notice the undeniable bulge pressing against my back...

3

LUKE

I wake up early, my eyes flickering to the warm sunlight piercing my cabin curtains. My body is still buzzing with the vivid memory of Claire from last night's dream. I throw off the sheets and make my way to the bathroom, turning on the shower. The warm water cascades over my skin, washing away the dirt and sweat from yesterday. My hand drifts down between my legs, my cock twitches against my fingers thinking of her. I reluctantly agreed to be a private guide for a solo trip through the savannah. I was hesitant at first, having dealt with ignorant and obnoxious clients in the past. But then she appeared, a real classy woman with the most gorgeous tits I have ever seen.

I step out of the shower and dry off. I dress quickly in khaki shorts and a cotton shirt, slipping on my hiking boots, and I make my way to the main building, grabbing a cup of coffee.

. . .

I lean against the hood of my 4x4, savoring the strong aroma of black coffee as I survey the vast savannah in front of me. I wait for her at our designated meeting spot, turned on at the thought of seeing her again. She is late. I knock on the door of her lodge.

When she finally opens the door, my breath catches in my throat. She wears a white lace nightgown that clung to her curves and leaves nothing to the imagination. My eyes can't help but linger on her full breasts, barely contained by the delicate fabric. Her long blonde hair is loose and flowing around her shoulders, with subtle hints of grey at her temples that only add to her beauty.

As I meet her gaze, I see her cheeks turn pink under my admiring stare. She smiles sweetly, and I feel lost in her captivating blue eyes. "Rise and shine," I say with a smirk, trying to hide how badly I want her right now. God, I want her.

Fuck, all I want is to pull her into my arms and make love to her on this very spot. But instead, I clear my throat and force myself to act normal. "We have 30 minutes before we need to leave. Get ready." I say, trying to keep my voice steady. Then, without another word, I return to my car.

The breeze ruffles in the air, carrying the scent of the African savannah - warm earth and fresh grass. I take a long sip of coffee, trying to contain my excitement. My heart races in my chest as she gets closer.

· · ·

"Good morning," she says softly. "I'm so sorry, I overslept."

I nod and hold out a hand to help her into the 4x4. Our hands brush as she takes it, my cock stirring in my pants. I can't believe how much just that tiny touch affects me.

She slides into the passenger seat, and I can't help but admire the way her lashes flutter when she blinks. When she leans over to fasten her seatbelt, my hand brushes against her knee, feeling the softness of her skin against mine. My cock hardens instantly, and I lick my lips. I start the engine, and we bounce along the dirt track, the truck throwing us against each other. Her scent envelops me, and I close my eyes, taking a deep breath.

The sun is rising, casting golden light across the expanse before us. As we drive through the park, I keep glancing at her out of the corner of his eye. The way she sits there, so close yet far away, drives me crazy. I want to make her mine and own her completely, to claim her as my own.

Suddenly, we catch sight of a pride of lions, their ferocious beauty making my pulse race. I pull over and hand her the binoculars. She leans forward, her breath hot against my neck as she peers through the lenses. I can feel the press of her soft breasts against my arm, and I try not to grunt in pleasure. Claire gasps beside me, her breath hitching. I don't care if it's just a sound; I wish it was me who made her react like that.

. . .

We drive off, my heartbeat pounds erratically in my chest, my cock throbbing against my zipper. I drive further into the park, spotting some elephants, giraffes, zebras, and wildlife. I park the car next to a big tree, and we get out, enjoying the beauty. I can't help but notice how she fits perfectly in this wild place - like she belongs here - with me. I lift the binoculars again and scan the horizon.

"Look! Over there!" I exclaim, pointing towards a herd of buffalo.

Dusk begins to fall, and we stop to make camp beneath endless stars. I prepare the bedding for the night and build a fire. Claire is shivering, and I instinctively wrap my arms around her to warm her up. She turns towards me and I loose control, my lips meet hers. She moans in pleasure, and I deepen the kiss, taking control of her mouth, our tongues dancing erotically as I slide my hand down her back, cupping her ass.

"I want to be inside you, Claire, feel your walls clenching around me. Let me fill you up, baby," I growl.

She nods frantically. It's just me and her under the stars.

I lay her down inside the sleeping bag and start unbuttoning her shirt and shorts. Her skin is heated under my fingers as I brush them down her belly, finding her wet and ready for me. The softness of her skin is an aphrodisiac, driving me wild. I push my hard length inside her slowly, feeling the tight heat engulf me. She gasps, breathless, eyes fluttering shut.

"Fuck you feel so good, Claire!"

I thrust slowly, deeply, feeling her wetness coating me. The rhythm grows faster and harder, our skin slapping together. Her breasts sway hypnotically as she meets my pace, her nipples tightening into hard nubs against my chest. I pull her hair, guiding her head back and exposing her neck. It's vulnerable and tempting, and I take it between my teeth, leaving a mark of possession. She responds by biting my shoulder and drawing blood.

"Naughty girl," I say, excited. "You need to be punished for that." I turn her around and fuck her from behind, her face down on the ground, her ass in the air. I slam myself into her deep, pushing with all my weight. She screams like a bitch in heat.

"You are mine now, Claire, "I growl as I cum inside her. "Mine."

4

CLAIRE

The sun falls below the horizon, coloring the sky in fiery hues of orange and crimson. Another day's adventure on the endless savanna folds into the night embrace. My heartbeat syncs with the distant roar of a lion, primal and untamed. Luke's hand, rough and calloused, clasps mine with possessive strength, his touch igniting a familiar trail of heat up my arm.

Breathless, I am caught between awe at the wilderness around us and the raw desire that Luke stokes within me each night. The vastness of the African plains mirrors the intensity of our nightly escapades—unrestrained, passionate, consuming.

I find myself standing before him, exposed, the last rays of sunlight kissing my skin. I feel vulnerable and insecure about the soft curves and fine lines that fifty years have etched onto my aging body. But Luke doesn't see the flaws that haunt my reflection in the mirror. To him, I am a goddess carved from the earth we walk upon, a creature to be worshipped and protected. His eyes trace my silhouette with such reverence as if every curve and scar speaks of a life well-lived, a sensuality earned rather than diminished by time. His gaze sweeps over me, heavy with an almost predatory hunger, and I shiver from anticipation.

He steps closer, the heat of his body promising another night of fervent love—a craving neither of us can sate—the wild call to us both. Nothing exists beyond the fierce grip of his hands and the promise of ecstasy that the African night offers.

But with each day that goes by, so does the countdown of days left in my African escape. Soon, this intoxicating rhythm will cease. The thought slices through me, sharp as the thorn bushes dotting the savanna.

I inhale deeply and draw in the scent of the dusk, trying to brand it into memory—arid earth, rich and potent, mingling with the subtle perfume of exotic flora. I let his strong, possessive hands caress me. His touch has become my lifeline, tethering me to moments of pure ecstasy where age and fear dissolve under the relentless African sun. How can I return to a world devoid of his hunger?

My heart clenches with longing and the bittersweet tang of impending solitude. I ache with the need to freeze time, to live in the suspended space between heartbeats where only our passion exists, fierce and unyielding as the land that cradles us.

But as the darkness swallows the savanna, I steel myself for the inevitable. It's time to go.

5

LUKE

I never knew fourteen days could pass this quickly. And, with each one, my feelings for Claire have deepened. I'm obsessed with her - her quick wit, shy smiles, and how she looks at me with those eyes. She stimulates me mentally and physically; her insecurities only make me want to protect her more.

I know I'm falling hard. It terrifies me. The ghosts of my past still haunt me. But Claire is worth it. I have seen her blossom and embrace her vulnerability, allowing me to love her fiercely and possessively. I feel the chains I've carried for so long loosening.

Claire's eyes are distant today. We both know what's coming - the end of her trip and possibly the end of us. We've avoided the topic. I take her hands, small and delicate in my rough grip.

. . .

"Stay with me," the words tumble out of my mouth. Her eyes widen in surprise. My heart pounds against my ribs. I'm terrified she'll refuse, but I know I have to try.

"Don't go back yet. I...I need you."There, I said it.

Claire's eyes search my face as if looking for any hint of insincerity. I hold her gaze steadily, allowing her to see the depth of my feelings.

"Luke, I...I don't know what to say," she whispers.

My heart sinks, but I plunge forward. "We have something here, something real. I've never felt this way about anyone before." I run my thumb gently over her knuckles. "Stay with me, just for a little while longer. We can take things slow and figure this out together. You know, years ..."

I see hesitation in her eyes, "Years?" she asks.

"Decades. It will take a long time to figure it out ..." I respond. Claire nods and grins from side to side, radiant.

"Is that a yes?" I ask, and she nods. I pull her into my arms, cradling her head against my chest as I breathe in the sweet floral scent of her hair. She is mine, and I can never let her go.

EPILOGUE

CLAIRE

The morning sun streams in through the open window, bathing our bed in a warm glow. Luke's arm is draped heavily over my waist, his breath tickling the back of my neck. I smile, remembering the passion of the night before, how he claimed me over and over again until I was spent and trembling.

These last three years with Luke have awakened the wild side within me. Now, I run toward every day, hungry for each new experience. Luke has shown me that surrender can be strength and that in giving myself fully to him, I have found myself.

I slip from Luke's embrace and pad naked across the room. The cold floor sends shivers up my spine. From the window, I can see the Cape Town harbor stretching out before me, the cries of seagulls mixing with the sounds of the waking city. My camera sits on the dresser, and I lift it gently, already composing the morning's first shot in my mind's eye.

My new book of photos is my latest venture, capturing the vibrancy and beauty of this place and its people. With each click of the shutter, I feel more alive.

I sense Luke stirring behind me. Soon, his arms will be around my waist, his lips grazing my shoulder, hungry again despite our long night of pleasure. And I will melt into him. This is my life now. I have been claimed, possessed, and in surrender, I have found my strength.

GET YOUR FREE EBOOK

Sign up the Laura (L.A.) Mariani mailing list for a FREE steamy romance.

You'll be the first to hear about new releases, exclusive offers, bonus content and all Laura's news. You can even email her back. She loves chatting with her readers!

To claim your free ebook visit:
https://laura-mariani-author.ck.page/freeshortstory

ABOUT THE AUTHOR

Laura (L.A.) Mariani is a best selling author of Short &
Steamy Romance |Where Alpha Males Meet Fierce Hero-
ines for Sweet Endings, your go-to author for captivating
romance tales that will sweep you off your feet and keep
you on the edge of your seat!

When Laura is not weaving stories of love, desire and
suspense, you'll find her exploring the vibrant streets of
London, drawing inspiration from its hidden corners and
bustling markets, or strolling through the charming streets
of Paris, savoring street food in Rome, or relaxing on a sun-
kissed beach in Bali, her journeys fuelling her creativity and
infuse her stories with wanderlust.

You can also follow her on

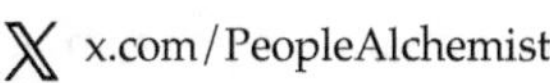

X x.com/PeopleAlchemist
instagram.com/lauramariani_author
facebook.com/lauramarianiauthor

AUTHOR'S NOTE

Thank you so much for reading **14 Days To Love.**

I hope you enjoyed the stories. A review would be much appreciated as it helps other readers discover the story. Or a few stars perhaps - the more the better ;-) !

Thank you.

Interesting facts

Romeo in Rome: the carbonara recipe is an adaptation of Luciano Monosillo's carbonara recipe (**Luciano Cucina Italiana** restaurant), Rome Carbonara King.

Marrakesh Magic: Throughout this short novella, the word Marrakesh has been spelled differently, depending on whether it is pronounced by Jean-Claude or Sarah. This was intentional.

"Marrakesh" is the common English spelling, whilst "Marrakech" is the spelling widely used in Francophone countries/by French people.

www.ingramcontent.com/pod-product-compliance
Lightning Source LLC
Chambersburg PA
CBHW051002180726
48291CB00006B/1935